"So. They left one of their number behind. Prepare to die, woman.

"I am Andrew Ross and this is my castle. Tell me quickly who you are and what you do here."

"My name is Gwenellen. My home is in a land known as the Mystical Kingdom."

That had him releasing her and taking a step back. "I've heard of such a place. All Highlanders have heard the tale. But it is no more than a myth."

"If it be a myth, than I am one, as well, but I assure you, sir, I am real."

All too real, Andrew thought as he was forced to absorb a strange rush of heat that nearly seared his flesh. He pulled away as though burned and looked down to see if she'd left a mark on him. Though his skin was without blemish, he could still feel the tingling all the way to his fingertips. "How do you come to be here? Have you brought witchcraft to this place?"

* * *

The Knight and the Seer
Harlequin Historical #678—October 2003

good

RUTH LANGAN

THE KNIGHT AND THE SEER

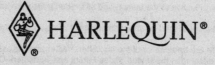

HARLEQUIN®

TORONTO • NEW YORK • LONDON
AMSTERDAM • PARIS • SYDNEY • HAMBURG
STOCKHOLM • ATHENS • TOKYO • MILAN • MADRID
PRAGUE • WARSAW • BUDAPEST • AUCKLAND

ISBN 0-373-29278-3

THE KNIGHT AND THE SEER

Visit us at www.eHarlequin.com

Printed in U.S.A.

Please address questions and book requests to:
Harlequin Reader Service
U.S.: 3010 Walden Ave., P.O. Box 1325, Buffalo, NY 14269
Canadian: P.O. Box 609, Fort Erie, Ont. L2A 5X3

For Patty, our gifted artist,
who colors all our lives with love.

And, of course, for Tom, who paints with laughter.

Prologue

Mystical Kingdom—1552

"Now stand right here, Jeremy." Nine-year-old Gwenellen, of the clan Drummond, helped the little troll onto a flat rock before taking several steps backward. She had the look of a pixie, with fine golden curls spilling down her back in tangles, and laughing eyes the color of warm honey. "You have to hold out your hands like this…" she lifted her hands, palms up and waited for him to do the same, "…so you don't miss any of the flowers I'm going to send you."

Catching the look of disbelief that passed between her older sisters, Kylia and Allegra, who were standing to one side, the little girl huffed out a breath. "I know what you're thinking. Just because I've made a few…missteps before, you think I can't ever get these spells to work. But this time I'll prove you wrong.''

"And if you don't?" Allegra, the oldest of the sisters at ten and three, had hair the color of fire and green eyes that danced with amusement as she studied the troll dressed in his top hat and frock coat, who looked like he'd rather be anywhere than here, as the object of her little sister's experiment. "Poor Jeremy is the one who'll find himself flying backward, or tumbling down a well."

"Aye." Kylia, a year younger than Allegra, with raven-black tresses and eyes the color of heather, nodded. "Or hanging from the very top of a tree, or sailing across the sky. And all because of your missteps."

Gwenellen's face grew redder with each mention of her many accidents. She was their despair and their delight. Despite her many failures, she never doubted that she would one day master the skills necessary to be a witch like her mother, grandmother and sisters.

The troll, Jeremy, was no bigger than a wee lad, his head barely reaching their shoulders. He claimed to have lived in the real world for more than a hundred years before making his home in the Mystical Kingdom with these lasses and their family. From the beginning he'd been especially fond of Gwenellen, whose sweet nature made it impossible not to love her, despite her imperfections. Though he wasn't known for his patience, he'd shown a great deal of restraint while the little girl practiced her spells and talents, usually with disastrous results.

"He was never hurt." Gwenellen shot a pleading look at the troll. "Tell them, Jeremy. None of my missteps ever caused you harm."

"So far." His voice resembled the croaking of a frog. "But be careful, my little friend. This time I'd prefer the petals to the thorns."

"Aye. I'll keep that in mind." She turned to her two sisters with a haughty look. "We'll just see who can conjure the prettiest roses in all the land."

Tossing her hair back from her face she lifted her arms heavenward and assumed an air of great concentration before beginning to chant the ancient words. Though she paused a number of times as her tongue twisted over an unfamiliar word or phrase, she doggedly continued to the end before calling out triumphantly, "I bid thee now, from thy sweet bower, send me down the loveliest flower."

A single angry dark cloud gathered overhead, followed by a rumble of thunder that brought Gwenellen's mother, Nola, and her grandmother, Wilona, racing across the meadow, with Bessie, the hunched old crone who was also part of their family, trailing behind. Everyone looked up at the sky expectantly just as the cloud opened up and spilled its contents over Jeremy.

Instead of flowers, they watched as he was covered

with a white, powdery substance that mounded around his feet, spilled over his top hat, coated his clothes, and sent him into a fit of sneezing.

Gwenellen stood perfectly still as the others raced to Jeremy's side and began to dust him off. As they did, Allegra and Kylia started giggling.

"You think this is amusing?" The little troll's ruddy face grew as dark as the storm cloud that had now blown away.

"It isn't you, Jeremy." Allegra dipped a finger into the powder and tasted it before falling into the grass, convulsed with laughter. "It's just that Gwenellen came so close, this time."

"Close?" The little girl was fighting tears. "How can you say such a thing? What I wanted was rose petals."

"Not roses. Flowers," Kylia said, between snorts of laughter. "You asked for the loveliest flower. And what you got was…" She could barely speak over the laughter. "What you got was flour. Fine, milled flour."

The two girls continued giggling while Jeremy stared in disgust at his top hat and frock coat, covered with white dust.

As for Gwenellen, she plunked herself down in the grass and rested her chin on her clenched fists, blinking back tears.

When the others had scattered, Wilona sat down beside her granddaughter, while Nola stood with her hands on her hips, regarding the two of them. "Another misstep, my darling?"

The little girl nodded. "These spells are so easy for the rest of you, Gram. Why are they so hard for me?"

The old woman drew her granddaughter close and pressed a kiss to the top of her head. "You just need time to uncover your gifts, Gwenellen."

"Aye. That's what Father said."

"Your father?" Wilona drew back and shot a glance at Nola. "When did he talk to you?"

"Last night. I was having trouble sleeping, because of that little...misstep I had yesterday." She steadfastly refused to call them mistakes, insisting that they were mere miscalculations.

Wilona thought about poor Jeremy, paddling furiously at the bottom of the well, and shouting at the top of his lungs to be rescued from Gwenellen's latest attempt at a spell. He would have hardly referred to it as anything but a catastrophe.

"Are you sure it was your father, my darling?"

Gwenellen nodded. "He looked so tall and handsome, with his plaid tossed over one shoulder, and the glint of a jeweled dirk at his waist."

Nola dropped to her knees and touched a hand to her daughter's arm. There was a new urgency to her voice. "What color were the jewels?"

"Deep, dark red, like blood, Mum. Except for the middle one, that was as green as Allegra's eyes."

The child turned to her grandmother. "And a lock of his dark hair spilled over his forehead just so." The little girl touched a finger to the old woman's brow.

The two women went very still. Gwenellen had just described her father perfectly, even though she'd never seen him, for he'd died before she was born. He was a mortal who had defied his clan to marry Nola, knowing she possessed powers that were frowned upon by his people. Yet theirs had been a true love-match, and until the day he died, he'd made her life unbelievably happy.

"What did your father say to you, lass?"

Gwenellen's smile returned. "He told me that I had a gift. A very special gift which no one else in the Mystical Kingdom possessed. He said that it could not be used here, though he didn't say why. But he told me that when I leave our kingdom and go into the world of mortals, it will hold me in good stead." She looked over and saw the way her grandmother was looking at her. "What is it, Gram? What's wrong?"

Wilona brushed her hand down the child's hair. "There's nothing wrong, my darling. Your father is right. Your gift is very special indeed. And one day, in the world of mortals, you'll discover just how important it is. Now go and make peace with Jeremy.

When the little girl skipped away, Wilona got to

her feet. "You know what this means, don't you, my daughter?"

Nola seemed almost reluctant to admit it, even to herself. "No wonder her gift isn't apparent here in the Mystical Kingdom, for there are no graves here."

"Aye. But in that other world, she will be able to speak with all their cherished dead."

"It is a rare and precious gift."

The older woman looked thoughtful. "And one that is often misunderstood."

"We must shield her, and see that she never strays from the Mystical Kingdom."

With a sigh Wilona drew her daughter close. "It's impossible to shield her from the world, my child. What we must do is help her find her strengths so that if she should ever find herself away from here, she'll be able to survive."

The object of their discussion danced across the meadow in search of her playmate. She would need a great deal more practice before being called a certified witch like her sisters. But it would happen, she vowed. She would just have to work a little harder.

And find a way to stay in Jeremy's good graces until she succeeded.

Chapter One

Mystical Highlands—1561

"Here now." Nola Drummond lay her hands upon her youngest daughter, Gwenellen, sprawled in the heather, looking dazed.

Seeing her daughter tumbling from the sky had started Nola's heart drumming like a runaway carriage. It was nothing new. It seemed to her she'd spent a lifetime worrying about this free spirit who was always getting herself into trouble. But every time it happened, her heart seemed to die a little. "Let me take care of your cuts first, child. That was a nasty fall you took."

"Aye." Gwenellen started to sit up, but when she saw the sky spinning in dizzying circles overhead, she fell back against the fragrant flowers and allowed her mother to ply her gifts of healing. "One minute I was riding Starlight past a bank of clouds…" She looked over to see her winged horse standing nearby, calmly nibbling grass. ''...and the next I was tumbling through space.''

''It wouldn't have anything to do with the fact that you were trying to beat Jeremy in a race again, would it?''

Gwenellen saw the little troll running to keep up with the brisk strides of her grandmother, Wilona, who wore a look of concern as she headed across the meadow toward them.

''Are you hurt, lass?'' Wilona tossed long silver hair back from her face and began to probe Gwenellen's wounds. ''Jeremy said you fell from Starlight's back in midair.''

''She was trying out a new spell that would let her fly.'' The troll's voice was a nervous, high-pitched croak. ''It's worked before. She was certain it would work again.''

''Certain. You're always so certain.'' There was something new in Nola's tone. Not just accusing, but something more, rising up to grab her by the throat. Terror? Despair? She turned back to her youngest daughter. ''You may be certain of this. One of these times those failed spells will get you into serious trouble.''

As always, Wilona tried to smooth things over between her daughter and granddaughter. ''Well, it seems there's been no harm done. I see nothing more than a few simple cuts and bruises.''

"You see, Mum?" Gwenellen sat up carefully and waited for the world to settle.

"You could have been killed." Nola got to her feet and shook down her skirts. "When will you learn that you can't keep taking these foolish risks without paying a price?" She turned to the troll. "Jeremy, you may as well unsaddle Starlight. Gwenellen will remain on the ground for the rest of the day."

Jeremy shot his friend a sympathetic wink as he turned away to see to the horses.

When Nola stalked away Gwenellen turned to Wilona. "Mum was furious."

"She worries over you."

"Oh, Gram. Why do I keep making all these foolish blunders?"

"It's called growing up, my darling." The older woman ran a hand over the silken curls that were now a mass of tangles. Such glorious golden hair, in rich contrast to those honey-brown eyes. Her grandmother was quite certain Gwenellen didn't have the faintest idea that she was a stunning beauty. How could she? There were no mirrors, except the smooth surface of the Enchanted Loch. And no one here in the Mystical Kingdom to reflect back her beauty.

"I'm never going to be grown up. Look at me. I'm ten and eight, and still can't heal wounds like Allegra, or cast spells like Kylia."

"You have your own special gifts, Gwenellen."

"What gifts? Oh. You mean talking with my father. But what good is that?"

"What good? I'll tell you. In that other world…"

"I don't care about that other world. Here, my spells fail more often than they succeed. I can't tame the weather." She gave her head a shake, sending fair curls dancing. "I can't even tame my hair." She covered her face with her hands. "I'm never going to be like you and Mum and Allegra and Kylia."

"That's true, my darling." Wilona got to her feet and drew her granddaughter up before gathering her close. "You'll never be like anyone but yourself. And that's exactly as it should be." She framed the pretty, heart-shaped face with her gnarled hands. "Listen to me, Gwenellen. Life is a journey. At times it's a grand adventure. At other times it can prove to be a bit of a challenge."

"Mine seems to be all challenge," Gwenellen muttered with a pout.

"Pay it no mind. What we see as mistakes are simply lessons we must learn as we travel through this world."

"Why then do I seem to have so many more lessons to learn than my sisters?"

Wilona smiled. "I haven't the answer to that, my darling. But this I know. You're very special to me. And one day you'll prove your value, not only to yourself, but to someone who will mean more to you than any you have known so far."

Gwenellen kissed her grandmother's cheek. "I know you mean to comfort me, Gram, by suggesting that I will one day have a man who loves me the way Merrick MacAndrew loves Allegra, and Grant MacCallum loves Kylia. But I have no interest in snagging a mortal man who will carry me off to his Highland fortress, so I may play mistress to his castle while he marches off to battle. I much prefer my life here in the Mystical Kingdom with you, Mum, Jeremy and Bessie."

"You say that now because you haven't yet met the man who will claim your heart."

"My heart is not to be bargained for." Gwenellen stepped back, feeling the return of her impish good nature. "I would, however, be very happy if I could perfect one good spell that would work every time I attempted it."

"Name one, my darling."

She thought a moment. "A spell that would let me fly."

"What need have you of flying, when you have Starlight to carry you wherever you choose?"

"Starlight can only carry me to the heavens and back. You and Mum can travel anywhere with but a thought."

Wilona laughed. "My darling, it's taken us a lifetime to learn to travel as we do. Be patient. In time it will come to you. In fact, it will probably happen when you least expect it. Now." She turned away.

"I promised Bessie I'd make up a batch of biscuits to go with her stew."

She started away, then paused and turned. "I believe it would greatly please your mother if you and Jeremy would bring home some berries from the forest for our dessert."

Gwenellen nodded. "You mean, it would go a long way toward making amends?"

Wilona smiled. "Aye. It wouldn't hurt."

"Very well." Gwenellen turned away. "Tell Bessie to whip some clotted cream to go with the berries."

"Here, Jeremy." Gwenellen handed the little troll a bucket and pointed to a row of bushes heavy with roseberries. Sweet as cherries, tart as raspberries, luscious as strawberries, without seeds or pits, they were a special treat that grew only in the Mystical Kingdom. "You get those in the lower branches and I'll pick the ones higher up."

They picked for several minutes in silence. Finally over a mouthful of berries Jeremy asked, "Are you certain you're all right, Gwenellen?"

"I'm fine. It was only my pride that was hurt."

"You're as fine and clever a witch as your sisters. You're just too ambitious for your own good. You ought to accept the gifts you have, and not worry about the others."

"Now you sound like Gram." Laughing, Gwenellen got to her feet and began to pick once more. "She says I can talk to the dead. That may be a fine gift, except that there are no dead here in our kingdom." She stood on tiptoe to reach a cluster of perfect berries. "Gram says I must keep on trying to find my other gifts, because each failure is simply another lesson to be learned."

"If that's so, you should be just about perfect by now."

"Aye." As she enjoyed his joke, Gwenellen's laughter rang on the air, as clear as a bell. Then she stood back, considering. "Maybe I am trying too hard. Perhaps the answer is to just relax a bit more, and play with a variety of spells, without regard to the outcome."

"Why not?" The little troll shrugged. "It's worth a try. Want to start with something simple now?"

Gwenellen looked around. Spying the juiciest berries at the very top of the bushes, she smiled. "I believe I'll try that flying spell again. Only this time if it fails, I won't have so far to fall."

Slipping the handle of the bucket over her wrist, she extended her arms and closed her eyes as she began to chant the ancient words. With each phrase the air grew softer, warmer. The birds and insects fell silent as clouds gathered overhead.

She could feel the sudden rush of air, billowing her skirts about her ankles as she became airborne.

Oh, it was just the nicest feeling in the world when a spell went the way it ought.

She opened her eyes, determined to pick the berries at the top of the bushes. To her horror she discovered that she was so high in the air, the Mystical Kingdom was little more than a dot on the landscape far below.

''Oh, no. This will never do.'' She closed her eyes and repeated the chant, reversing the words in the hope that it would take her back to the beginning. But when she opened her eyes she saw fields and forests, mountains and rivers, moving below her in a blur of dizzying movement that had her feeling more than a little light-headed.

Where had she gone wrong? She went over the chant in her mind, hoping to speak the words that would break this spell.

Home. She needed to get back home.

To keep from being sick she closed her eyes and concentrated all her energy on her home, her family. She visualized each of them in her mind. Mum, at her loom, weaving the beautiful cloth that was unlike any seen by mortals. So soft, so fine, it could have been spun by angels. Gram, taking perfectly-browned biscuits from the hearth, and slathering them with freshly-churned butter, and honey fresh from the comb. Old Bessie, a soiled apron tied around her ample middle, wooden spoon in hand, stirring the most fragrant stew in her blackened kettle. And Jeremy, probably running as fast as his little legs could carry him back to their cottage, to relay news of her latest blunder.

Oh dear, she thought. Now they would all know that she had once again failed.

Perhaps, if she concentrated very hard, she could make it back before Mum had time to worry.

As if by magic she could feel herself descending. With a smile she opened her eyes just in time to see the ground coming up toward her. This time, instead of crashing into a meadow of heather, she drifted to earth and landed without mishap.

"Well, that's better." She looked around for Jeremy.

But instead of the roseberry bushes, she found herself standing amid the smoldering rubble inside some sort of fortress. The space around her was littered with charred timbers and bits and pieces of furniture and tapestries.

The stench of smoke and death was all around her, filling her lungs until she found herself coughing and retching. When the fit of coughing passed, she straightened. Hearing a footfall she turned.

And found herself looking into the eyes of a man whose features were twisted into a mask of fury.

In his hand was a sword which he lifted until it was pointed directly at her heart.

"So. They left one of their number behind." His voice was a low rumble of anger. "Prepare to die, woman."

Chapter Two

Gwenellen struggled to think of a spell. Any spell that might freeze this stranger before he could run her through. But her mind went completely blank. All she could think to do was hold her hands out in front of her, as though they could somehow stop the path of a sword that was nearly as big as she.

He stared in suspicion at the bucket on her arm. "What weapons are you hiding in there?"

"Hi...?" She swallowed and tried again. "Hiding? I hide nothing, sir. I was out picking berries."

"Here?" He swung a hand to indicate the charred rubble. "You expect me to believe you were picking berries and didn't realize you'd wandered into my family fortress?"

"This is...yours?"

He nodded, eyes narrowed on her. "If you lived in the village, you would know of this place, for I am Andrew Ross, and this castle is known as Ross

Abbey. My ancestors have been here for hundreds of years.'' When he saw no flicker of recognition in her eyes he hissed out a breath of impatience. ''Tell me quickly who you are and what you do here.''

''My name is Gwenellen, of the clan Drummond. My home is in a land known as the Mystical Kingdom.''

That had him taking a step back. ''I've heard of such a place. All Highlanders have heard the tale. Of the mortal, Kenneth Drummond, who married a witch, then gave his life to save hers. Of the dragon that guards the Enchanted Loch. Of the Forest of Darkness that lies between it and the rest of the Highlands. But it is no more than a myth.''

''If it be a myth, than I am one, as well.'' When she lowered her bucket to show him the berries inside, he seemed unconvinced. She reached out a hand to touch his arm. ''I assure you, sir, like these berries, I am real.''

All too real, he thought, as he was forced to absorb a strange rush of heat that nearly seared his flesh. He pulled away as though burned and looked down to see if she'd left a mark on him. Though his skin was without blemish, he could still feel the tingling all the way to his fingertips. ''How do you come to be here?''

She shook her head. ''I know not. One moment I was picking berries, the next I was standing here before you, as you now see me.''

"Perhaps you've been bewitched. Have you brought witchcraft to this place?"

She paused. "In your land it is called witchcraft. In my kingdom we are simply practicing the gifts of the ancient ones. My sisters, my mother and my grandmother have many gifts."

Again she saw his look of disbelief. "What of you, woman? What are your gifts?"

"I fear I'm not much good at the art of mysticism. But I'm very good at falling from the sky. And getting lost, it seems." She started to laugh, then thought better of it when she saw his frown. "I have no idea what my gifts might be, nor why I'm here."

"Nor do I." He abruptly turned away and stared at the smoldering ruins of his home. "Leave me. For I have graves to dig and loved ones to bury."

"I could help."

"I doubt one small female could be of much help. Unless you can conjure my enemy and have him kneel before me to face my sword, for he will surely pay for destroying everything I hold dear. Leave me now." He strode away, leaving her standing alone in the smoke and ashes.

She watched as he began tossing aside charred timbers, unmindful of the burns he was forced to endure to his hands. Like a madman he pawed through the ruins. Suddenly he dropped to his knees and lifted the body of a man whose hand was still clutching a sword.

"Oh, Father." His voice was a low rasp of pain mingled with fury. "How has it all come to this? I was such a fool. If only I'd stayed."

"Nay." The word was little more than a whisper on the wind. But Gwenellen heard it as clearly as though she had her ear pressed to the old man's lips. *"Ye mustn't blame ye'rself. I was the fool. Such a fool."*

"My fault." Andrew rocked the lifeless body in his arms. "If I hadn't been so quick to leave. But how could I stay, knowing what you were about to do? How?"

There was a long moment of silence, followed by a deep sigh.

"Ye must help me help him, lass. Will ye do that?"

Again the whisper, louder this time, and Gwenellen looked over, seeing the look of shock and grief in Andrew's eyes. Why was he grieving, when his father was still here? Could he not hear what she heard so clearly?

"Don't ye see, lass? I can no longer speak to him. But I can speak with ye. And ye can be the bridge between my world and his."

When the realization came, Gwenellen was so startled, she could do nothing more than stare in stunned surprise. Andrew was grieving because his father was no longer here. The old man truly had slipped away to that other world. As her own father had, before she was born. And yet this man, like her father, could communicate with her. Unlike others, she felt no barrier between herself and that other world. His words were as clear, as plain, as the one who held him in his arms.

Her grandmother's words came to her. Everything in life happens for a reason. Even when things are seen as problems, they are merely lessons which must be learned.

This, then, was one of her true gifts. Hadn't her grandmother said as much? But because it had seemed so natural to talk to her father, she'd dismissed her grandmother's words. Now, after all these years of uncertainty, it was being brought back to her more clearly than ever.

"I'll...do what I can, sir."

Andrew didn't hear her as he lifted his father's lifeless body in his arms and carried it through the rubble to a distant corner of the garden, where he began digging a grave.

Setting aside her bucket, Gwenellen imitated Andrew Ross by digging through the rubble, in search of others who might need her gift.

A short time later she heard Andrew cry out and looked over to see him unrolling a parchment that had been affixed to the center of a table by the blade of a knife. After reading it he gave a snarl of anger and crushed the parchment in his clenched fist.

Gwenellen hurried over to stand beside him. "What is it? What have you found?"

He seemed almost dazed, as though only vaguely aware of her presence beside him. "It's as I'd suspected. Fergus Logan. There has been enmity between his clan and ours from the time of our ancestors. And now he's taken his vengeance by not only boasting of killing my father, but of taking his wife as hostage." His black mood darkened with every word. "This time his vile deeds will not go unpunished."

"What will you do?"

He turned away without another word.

In silence he returned to the rubble with a renewed sense of urgency.

The setting sun cast the land in deep purple shadows. Gwenellen sat on a log, and watched as Andrew smoothed the dirt over the last grave and knelt to whisper a prayer. Around them were a score of fresh mounds, each of them marking the grave of one of the beloved members of his household.

Each of them had spoken to her. An introduction. A request to carry words to family and friends left behind. Occasionally an apology for some hurt they'd failed to heal before leaving this world.

So many voices calling out to her. Filling her mind. Touching her heart. At first it had seemed a babble of voices, until she'd begun to sort them out, giving each a bit of her time before moving on to the next. She'd listened to all, and had given her word to do what she could to ease the pain of those who were grieving. But the one that had touched her the deepest had been Andrew's father, who expressed a fear that anger and bitterness would cloud his son's judgment.

Andrew knelt a moment longer in prayer before getting to his feet. When he turned, he seemed surprised to see her.

"Why are you still here, woman?"

"I thought..." The fierceness of the man frightened her. Still, she couldn't put aside the wishes expressed so eloquently by his dead father. "I thought I would stay until all were buried."

"You've been here all this time?" Andrew had been so locked in his own grief and anger he'd barely noticed her throughout the day. Now he realized that she, like him, must be beyond exhaustion.

He looked down at her, noting the dirt that stained her fine gown and lovely face. Then he caught sight of the blisters on her hands and his frown deepened as he caught them, holding them up for his inspection. "Little fool. What have you done?"

Embarrassed, she tried to snatch her hands away, but he held them fast and looked into her eyes. "When did you last eat?"

She shrugged, aware of a strange tingling along her arms. Was it because of his touch? Or was it merely the result of the blisters? "I had some berries while still in my homeland." Had it been hours?

Days? Time was so different here in the land of mortals.

"Come with me." He helped her up and led her to where his horse was tethered.

"Where are we going?"

He lifted her into the saddle and pulled himself up behind her before catching the reins. "There's a tavern in the village. I'll see that you're fed and given shelter until you can be returned to your home."

She trembled at the feel of his arms around her. There was a strange warmth where his hand, holding the reins, rested at her hip. "And you, sir?"

His breath stung her cheek. "There'll be no rest for me until the one who did this cruel deed answers to my sword."

The passion in his tone sent shivers along her spine, but Gwenellen remained silent about the words spoken by his father. It would be best if she waited awhile, and pondered the proper way to tell him of this strange new gift she'd discovered within herself. In truth, she feared his reaction. He seemed a simple, straightforward man of the sword. What if he refused to accept the fact that she had actually spoken with the dead?

They rode through Highland forests, across deep chasms filled with tumbling water, and along narrow winding trails until they reached the village far below. As they approached, the candlelight flickering in windows was a welcoming sight. Outside the tavern, horses blew and stomped in the night air that had cooled considerably.

Andrew slid from the back of his mount and tied the reins before lifting Gwenellen from the saddle. Again she felt the strength in him as he lifted her without effort and led the way inside. As soon as they stepped through the doorway, the chorus of voices in the public room fell silent.

"Andrew. Welcome home." The tavern owner hurried over to greet him. Seeing Andrew's charred tunic and blistered hands, he looked alarmed. "What has happened to you?"

"I returned home to find the fortress burned, and all who dwelled within it dead, Duncan."

At his words, the men were on their feet, gathering around him with a low buzz of speculation.

"Did no one see a roving band of warriors, Duncan?"

The old man shook his head sadly. "I fear not. I confess that I saw smoke in the distance, and suspected it might be the fires of invaders, who've been spotted in the hills. But your father had an army of warriors at the keep. I'd have thought them adequate for any threat."

"As did I." Andrew nodded. "Alas, I was mistaken, for all have perished."

"Did no one survive?"

"One." Andrew removed the rolled parchment from his tunic. "This was left behind."

Aloud the tavern owner identified the seal. "It is from Fergus Logan, of the north." In somber tones he read, "We have the mistress of Ross Abbey. You will kneel in submission, or forfeit her life."

That created an even greater buzz of speculation among the tavern guests.

Duncan's voice rose above the din. "Your father's wife is now in the hands of his most hated enemy. How soon will you ride to his stronghold?"

"As quickly as I can raise an army. I'll need a villager to ride to Edinburgh with a missive to my warriors."

The tavern owner signaled to a youth, who stepped forward. Andrew scrawled a message on parchment, rolled it and handed it to the youth, along with a coin. "You're to go directly to Holyroodhouse and ask for Drymen MacLean."

"Aye." The lad pocketed the coin and hurried out the door.

Andrew gave a weary sigh. "The lady and I require a meal to refresh ourselves, Duncan." He glanced down at the soot staining his hands and tunic. "We'll also need rooms for the night, and water to bathe."

The innkeeper shouted for a serving wench. Minutes later a pink-cheeked lass hurried over. "Blythe will show you to your sleeping chambers, and will see that you have water for bathing." He nodded toward a small, private room off to one side.

"You'll find your meal awaiting you there whenever you're ready."

Andrew pressed some gold coins into the man's hand. "Also, if you could provide us with some clean garments, the lady and I would be grateful."

The tavern owner studied the gold and chuckled. "For this much you could have the clothes off our backs."

Andrew managed a weak smile. "That won't be necessary, Duncan. Just so they're clean and warm, until our own garments can be washed."

"Blythe will see to it." The older man turned to the wench. "After you show the gentleman and lady to their chambers, find my wife in the kitchen and tell her what they require."

The servant gave a quick nod of her head before leading the way up the stairs.

On the second floor she paused to open a door and stepped aside, saying, "I hope this room suits the lady."

Andrew looked around, noting the clean bed linens, and a cozy fire burning on the hearth. He arched a brow at Gwenellen, who nodded her approval.

"This is fine. You'll see to some warm water and clean clothes for the lady?"

"Aye, sir." She stepped out and led the way to a room across the hall. "Will this suit you?"

In his weariness he barely glanced at it. "It will be fine. Thank you."

When his door closed, Gwenellen stepped inside her room and moved slowly around, standing on tiptoe to peek out the high narrow window at a small garden below. Then she moved to the fire, pausing to extend her hands to the heat. Minutes later a knock on the door announced the arrival of several servants bearing a small round tub and buckets of warm water, as well as an armload of clothing.

When they were gone, Gwenellen removed her soiled clothes and sank gratefully into the warm water. As she soaked away the grime she thought about all that had transpired this day.

Was she meant to stay in this place and offer to help Andrew Ross? Or should she slip into the darkened garden below and attempt a few spells that might return her to the safety of the Mystical Kingdom? Of course, she'd had little luck with spells in the past. The next one might take her to a den of thieves. Or possibly to some distant star. There was no telling where she might land.

At the moment, the wisest choice would seem to be to do nothing. If she remained here, she had an opportunity to use her gifts for good. Gifts that seemed to do her no good at all in her kingdom.

''Oh, Father.'' She stood, dripping water, and wrapped herself in linen before stepping from the tub. ''Is this where I'm meant to be?''

Just then there was a hiss and snap on the hearth, and Gwenellen looked over to see a puff of smoke rising from the fire. As she watched, the smoke took on the form of her father.

"Welcome to my world, my daughter." His voice was like the sigh of the wind.

"I've seen little of it, but what I've seen isn't so different from our kingdom."

"There are good people here. And some, as you've witnessed by the destruction at Ross Abbey, who are not so good. Though it is not the paradise you left behind, there is great beauty here. It was always my wish that my children would travel comfortably between their world and mine."

"Then I'm happy to be here, Father, and learn more of your world." She started toward him, eager to embrace the man she'd learned to love, not only through his visits, but from the tales told her by her mother.

When she reached out her arms, he backed away. "My greatest regret is that I have never been able to hold you, my child."

His image faded, leaving nothing but a wisp of smoke, drifting toward the ceiling. And the lingering scent of her father that filled her with an odd sense of peace. For now, at least, she would do as her father wished and remain in this strange new land. And pray that it would prove to be less forbidding than her first glimpse had shown it to be.

Chapter Three

Dressed in a borrowed gown of bleached wool, and wearing a threadbare shawl around her shoulders, Gwenellen made her way down the stairs toward the small dining room. Inside she found Andrew Ross standing alone, staring into the flames of the fire. In his hand was a tankard of ale. When he turned toward her, she could see the pain of grief in his eyes. She found herself wondering what it would be like to find all those she loved dead upon her return. It was too horrible to contemplate, and she wished with all her heart that she could ease his suffering.

He quickly pulled himself together and struggled to be civil. "Will you have some ale to warm you, my lady?"

"Aye. Thank you." She waited while he filled a tankard and handed it to her.

When their fingers brushed, she absorbed the quick rush of heat and looked up with alarm. Had he felt it, too? She'd never felt anything like this in her kingdom. It must be something that could only be experienced in the mortal world.

He was already turning away, making it impossible to look into his eyes. She watched as he walked to the fireplace and stood in silence.

"I'm sorry for your loss." The words seemed so inadequate, but she couldn't think of anything else to say.

When he remained silent she cleared her throat. "Were you gone from your home a long time?"

He lifted his head and seemed to struggle to pull himself back from a dark place within. "I left the Highlands for Edinburgh less than a fortnight ago."

"What took you to Edinburgh?"

"I received a missive from the queen requesting my company at court." He spoke almost to himself. "It's as though my enemies were merely waiting for me to leave, in order to do their deeds."

"You think your enemy knew your fortress was vulnerable?"

"I know not." He looked up when a servant entered and began setting a table with fresh linen and silver. A second wench began arranging a platter of sliced mutton on the table, along with bowls of broth and a loaf of bread warm from the oven.

When the servant was finished she turned. "Mistress MacIntosh will send tea and pudding when you ring, sir."

"Thank you." He drained his goblet and waited until the wench left before holding a chair for Gwenellen. He took the seat across from her and held the platter while she helped herself to meat.

His gaze narrowed on her hands. "What happened to your blisters?"

Feeling self-conscious she lowered her hands to her lap. "I...worked a spell."

"You expect me to believe that?" He reached over and caught her hands, holding them palms up for his inspection.

There it was again. That quick rush of heat, and then the strange tingling that had her drawing back in alarm.

"I demand proof." He thrust his hands toward her. "Use the spell on mine."

She was already shaking her head. "That wouldn't be wise."

"Because it's all a lie?"

"Nay. But...it might go awry." She gave an embarrassed laugh. "Whenever I try my spells on poor Jeremy, he never knows what might happen. One time he found himself at the very top of a tree. Another time at the bottom of a well."

"Is Jeremy your husband?"

Again that soft, musical laugh that wrapped itself around his heart in a way that he found puzzling. "Jeremy is a troll who lives with us in the Mystical Kingdom."

"A troll?" He arched a brow. "Now I know you're having fun with me."

"Nay. I assure you. He is more than ten score years."

"No one lives more than a hundred years."

"No one in your world, perhaps." Seeing that he had no intention of withdrawing his hands, she gave a long sigh. "Just so you know that I tried to give you fair warning."

She kneaded his hands between both of hers, moving her thumb and fingers over his, while she began to chant.

Andrew was forced to absorb a sudden shaft of heat as her fingers slowly moved over his. Heat that went straight to his loins. As if that weren't enough, he felt a momentary thrill at the sound of that soft, breathy voice as she began to chant.

There was something about this woman. By firelight, her skin was as pale as alabaster, her eyes gleaming golden like a cat's. Her hair, the color of palest ale, fell in silken curls to below her waist. He had a compelling desire to plunge his hands into her hair, to see if it could be as soft as it looked. But that would be dangerous. For all he knew, she could have been sent by his enemies to lull him into a false sense of security. Besides, with all that had happened, he was hardly in a mood to have his mind muddled by some charming female.

Suddenly the chanting ceased and her eyes widened. ''I command you, as all things begin, to heal these wounds and make new this skin.''

At her words, something flew through the air and landed with a crash in the middle of the table, sending meat and gravy spilling across the linen cloth.

Both Gwenellen and Andrew pushed back from the table, staring at the resulting mess with matching looks of shock.

Then, as the truth dawned, Gwenellen's cheeks grew bright pink. ''I wanted this man's skin made new. Not a new skin.'' She picked up the odd thing that had intruded and muttered, ''It appears to be kidskin, or perhaps a lambskin.''

Andrew plucked it from her hands to study it by the light of the fire. ''I believe it's a pig's bladder.''

As Gwenellen blushed in embarrassment, the corners of Andrew's mouth curved upward. He wanted very much to laugh, but he knew it would only add to her humiliation. Still, the absurdity of it had him covering his mouth with his hand and coughing several times before turning back to her.

''I'm…'' Seeing what she thought was a scowl, she could hardly get the words out. ''I'm truly sorry. But I did warn you that my spells often went awry.''

''So you did. But I must admit I wasn't quite prepared for a pig's bladder in the middle of our table.'' He lifted a decanter, filling both their tankards. ''Let's ignore this…minor interruption and try to enjoy our meal.''

Humbled, Gwenellen took a bite of warm bread and made an attempt to get the man's mind off her blunder. "What did the queen ask of you when you went to Edinburgh?"

"Her Majesty is feeling put upon by many who want her to share the power of the throne. She requires a few trusted friends to counsel her on matters of church and state."

"And are you one of the queen's trusted friends?"

"My family has long been aligned with hers. Now that she has returned from France to claim her rightful place upon the throne, she is feeling besieged from all sides. But, though I was flattered by her trust, and eager to see her succeed, I have no desire to live anywhere but here in the Highlands. Alas, I arrived home too late."

"Do you believe someone alerted your enemy to your absence?"

He nodded. "How else to explain what happened?"

"And now your enemy has your stepmother."

"Sabrina." There was something about the way he spoke her name that had Gwenellen looking at him closely.

"Do you think she is still alive?"

"It would serve no purpose to kill her. Logan has long desired a war between us. My father resisted, believing it would drain our clan. Now, with Sabrina as bait, we'll have no choice but to do battle with those who covet our land, our flocks, our people."

"Would you surrender all in order to save her?"

He didn't answer directly. Instead he seemed to turn inward for a moment before choosing his words carefully. "I am a warrior. I will do what I must to avenge the death of my father."

"What will you do for an army?"

He gave a mirthless laugh. "My bravest and strongest warriors were left in Edinburgh, to guard the queen. Until they return, what I have left is a village of old men, and women and children."

"I could stay and help." She spoke the words softly.

"You? And how will you help? Will you cast a spell upon my enemies?"

She knew her cheeks were coloring again. She could feel the heat burning. She looked down, avoiding his eyes. "I can try."

"I'm sorry." Again that hint of laughter, though he managed to hold it inside. "I don't believe a pig's bladder will do much harm to my enemies. But I do thank you, my lady."

She felt the sting of his rejection. He thought her puny attempt at a spell was laughable.

Andrew had already dismissed her as he reached for the bell, convincing himself that there had been no blisters on her hands. In his grief, he'd only imagined them. He was certain of it.

Minutes later the little servant entered and began pouring tea and spooning pudding into dishes.

When the servant took her leave, Gwenellen tasted, then smiled. "It isn't as good as Bessie's, but it's still quite tasty."

"And who is Bessie? Another troll?"

Gwenellen's smile faded at his mocking tone. "A hunched old woman who lives in our kingdom. She once lived in your world, but because of the way she looks, she was often ridiculed. When she had the opportunity to leave this world and live with us in the Mystical Kingdom, she was most eager to do so."

"I hardly blame her." Andrew found himself fascinated with a strand of honey hair that dipped over one eye. It begged to be touched. With an effort he looked away. "There are many in my world who are cruel to those who are small, or weak or different." He set aside his half-eaten sweet. "If there is such a place as the Mystical Kingdom, I can understand why you and your family would choose to live there."

"Though I know you don't believe me, it truly does exist. I'm too young to remember, but I'm told that when we lived in your world our lives were threatened because we practiced the old ways. There were many who feared us, and wanted us put away."

"That seems to be our way of things." Ignoring the tea he reached for his goblet and emptied it, then pushed away from the table and stalked to the fireplace, where he stared in silence for many minutes. At last he turned and held her chair. "Come. After the day we've put in, we both have need of our rest."

He opened the door and allowed her to precede him before following her up the stairs.

Outside the door to her chambers he paused. "Despite the fact that your spell failed, I do thank you, my lady, for all that you did for me this day."

"You are most welcome, sir."

"As for your witchcraft..." He paused, then decided she'd suffered enough for her mistake. "I hope you'll take some time before trying another of your spells."

"As you wish." Gwenellen's smile faded when she suddenly felt his hand at her shoulder.

Startled, she turned back.

"Forgive me, my lady. I meant no offense."

"None taken."

But he could see that he'd hurt her. Her lips had already turned into a pretty little pout that held his gaze even when he tried to look away.

Without thinking he lifted her hands to his lips. "It would seem my grief has robbed me of my humanity. Even at my best, my mouth has always worked ahead of my brain. It is my great weakness." He brushed a kiss over the back of one hand, then the other, and experienced the most amazing rush of feeling. As though he'd just stepped off a high, steep cliff and was crashing to earth.

As for Gwenellen, the mere press of his lips to her flesh had her heart fluttering in her chest like a caged bird. Wide-eyed, speechless, she looked up at him just in time to catch the glint of something dark and dangerous that had crept into his eyes.

With reluctance he released her hands and started to back away. With no warning he caught her roughly by the upper arms, drawing her close.

Against her lips he muttered, "Woman, what have you done to me?"

Gwenellen had never in her life been caught by such surprise. One moment she'd been thinking about slapping his arrogant face. The next, her mind was wiped clear of all thought. It was impossible to think while those warm, clever lips were skimming hers. While those big calloused hands were gliding down her back, setting fires everywhere they touched. The very blood in her veins seemed to heat and thicken, until it flowed like molten lava. Her lips softened and warmed to him, while deep inside she felt a tug unlike anything she'd ever known.

Andrew absorbed a series of shocks. His body was suddenly alive with need. All his senses were sharpened. He could taste her. So sweet and exotic, it made his head swim. A taste that had him hungry for more. The woman scent of her filled him until he was drowning in her. He could feel her in every part of his body.

He hadn't meant for this to happen. But now that his hands were on her, his lips moving over hers, there was no stopping it.

There was such innocence here. He swallowed back her little gasp of surprise and took the kiss deeper, until he felt her lean into him and offer more.

His hands were in her hair. It was as soft as he'd imagined. Finer than the finest silk. His mouth whispered over her lips, her face, the tip of her nose, before returning to claim her lips once more.

Andrew knew he'd overstepped his bounds. It was clear from the hesitant way she responded that she'd never experienced such a thing before. And yet he couldn't resist. Not when her lips were so sweet. Not when her body was leaning into his, making him achingly aware of how perfectly she fit against him. The tug of desire was shocking in its intensity. The thought of filling himself with all that sweetness was almost overpowering.

When she sighed he breathed her in and allowed himself the pleasure of one last lingering kiss. Then, calling on all his willpower, he lifted his head and took a step back.

His tone, when he finally spoke, was gruff, mirroring the confusion he felt. Had this female bewitched him? What else could explain what had just happened between them? His father was barely cold in his grave, Sabrina was being held captive, and he was allowing himself to dally with a...witch. "I'll arrange for someone in the village to return you to your kingdom on the morrow."

"Return me? But I..."

He held up a hand to silence her protest. "I realize you would prefer one of your...spells, but I cannot leave your safety to chance. I owe you that much, at least, for the help you gave me this day. Be prepared to leave at first light."

He held her door, giving her no choice but to step inside. Gwenellen prayed her legs wouldn't fail her. Closing the door, she leaned weakly against it and listened as the door across the hallway closed.

Crossing the room she sank down on the edge of the bed. "Oh, Father. What am I to do now? Andrew doesn't want my help. He wants me to leave. And why not? I must seem the silliest of fools with that clumsy spell that went awry. And then that...kiss." It had seemed so much more than a kiss, but she thought it best not to mention that to her father. "How can I stay and help him now? How can I possibly challenge the will of this man?"

She waited for her father's words of wisdom. Instead there was only silence that seemed to close in around her, leaving her feeling lost and abandoned.

At last, desperate for sleep, she undressed quickly and climbed beneath the covers.

As she drifted into sleep, her dreams were filled

with visions of a tall, handsome warrior whose touch did strange things to her body, and whose gruff voice did strange things to her heart. But this was no sweet charmer. This was an angry warrior whose heart would be closed to even the most elaborate spells.

Though it saddened her, it would be best if she did as he'd ordered, and took her leave of this place on the morrow. There was safety in the Mystical Kingdom. Here in his land, there was only danger and deception. Some of the danger came from mortals bent on destroying one another.

But, she realized, there was also another kind of danger. One that was much more alluring. For which she had no name. And against which she had no defense.

Chapter Four

At the sound of masculine voices drifting from below stairs, Gwenellen stirred in her bed. How strange, after a lifetime of hearing only women, and, of course, Jeremy's croaking, to hear that low murmur that was so different.

She'd been strangely affected by Andrew's voice when first she'd heard it. Even though his words had been flung as a threat, there had been something about that deep timbre that had touched something inside her. Was it the similarity to her father's voice? Or was it just so different from the voices she'd grown accustomed to? Whatever the reason, she seemed mesmerized whenever he spoke.

She stepped out of bed and found her own clothes, freshly washed and carefully folded on a small chest. All sign of soot and ash had been scrubbed away. Even her kid boots were polished to a high shine.

She dressed quickly and ran her hands through the

tangles of her hair, doing her best to smooth it before making her way down to the public room. Inside there were half a dozen villagers breaking their morning fast. They eyed her with interest as they continued to eat.

"Ah, good morrow, my lady." Duncan, the tavern owner, hurried over and poured a mug of steaming tea. "May I offer you some mutton?"

"Thank you." She glanced around. "Has Andrew Ross awakened yet?"

"Oh aye. He was up at dawn, eager to begin work on his fortress." He paused. "He said that you would be leaving, my lady. In fact, he left a pouch of gold as payment to my wife's brother, William, who agreed to accompany you."

His words left her oddly deflated. She'd been so looking forward to seeing Andrew again. To hearing his voice, just once more, before being returned to her kingdom. She'd thought that if she could reason with him, she might be able to persuade him to allow her to remain, at least for a little while longer.

Still, why did she need his permission to remain here?

She gave the tavern owner her sweetest smile. "Tell William I'm grateful for his kind offer, but I've decided to stay."

"That's most generous of you, my lady. Will you be helping at the abbey?"

Before she could think of a reply Duncan nodded

toward the men at a nearby table. "The laird has offered work to anyone in the village who can spare the time from their flocks and crops. As soon as they've eaten, all of these men will be driving their teams up to Ross Abbey."

Without taking time to think about the consequences, she asked, "Would you ask if I might ride along?"

Duncan returned her smile. "I'm sure any one of these men would be happy to take you."

Minutes later a woman approached bearing a loaf of freshly-baked bread. Her hair was untidy, a sheen on her face from the heat of the kitchen. "Good morrow, my lady." She set down the bread and began to slice it. "I'm Mary, Duncan's wife."

"Good morrow, Mary. My name is Gwenellen, of the clan Drummond."

"My husband told me about you. He said you'd arrived last night with the laird's son." She gave her a long, steady look. "How is it that you and Andrew know each other?"

"We first met at his castle." Gwenellen decided not to try to explain further, and was delighted when the woman seemed to accept her answer as sufficient.

"I hope your clothes were cleaned to your satisfaction, my lady."

"Aye. I thank you."

The woman leaned close, keeping her voice low. "I pride myself on my dressmaking skills, but I confess, I've never seen a gown so fine as yours. Who did the weaving of this cloth?''

''My mother is the weaver.''

''The cloth is so fine, she could even dress the queen.''

Gwenellen's smile was radiant. ''I do thank you, Mary. I've always thought my mother had a rare talent, but it's nice to hear it from a stranger's lips as well.''

''Andrew said you'd be returning to your home, my lady.''

Gwenellen hesitated for only a second. ''I believe I shall stay in your lovely village awhile.''

''We're honored.'' The woman set a second slice of bread in front of Gwenellen, and as an afterthought offered a dab of honey before moving on to the next table.

At her kind gesture, Gwenellen couldn't help but smile. Perhaps this world wasn't so different from her own after all. At least they indulged their love of sweets.

She bent to her breakfast, intent upon being ready to leave whenever the villagers beckoned. After all, what would be the harm of remaining here for another day or two? She'd already had a taste of Andrew's anger. Though she'd been alarmed and more than a little afraid, she'd survived. She would survive another bout of temper. And if he should banish her, at least she'd have the satisfaction of having tried.

* * *

Andrew hauled the smoldering timber outside and placed it in the growing pile. Already more than a dozen villagers had arrived to lend a hand, with the promise of more when their farm chores had been tended.

Though the damage to the fortress had been extensive, he'd been pleased to discover by the light of morning that much of it could be salvaged. Because so much of the building was made of stone, the outer shell was sound. Fires had been set inside the castle area, torching the tapestries that had once lined the walls, destroying most of the wooden beams and much of the furniture.

Such things could be replaced, he reminded himself grimly. And would be. But the things that mattered most in his life could never be restored. He felt again the twin tugs of pain and guilt. Pain at the loss of his father and loyal servants who had been with his family for generations. Guilt that he and his father had parted in such anger. Now he must put aside his anger at his father and direct it against his enemy.

He silently vowed that the one who did this cruel thing would be caught and punished.

At the clatter of horses and carts he looked over to see more villagers arriving. In their midst sat Gwenellen, talking and laughing with the women as though she'd known them all her life.

His frown deepened as he stalked over to confront her. "Woman, what brings you here?"

"I wish to help."

His voice lowered, for her ears alone. "I warned you. I can't see to your safety."

"Then I'll just have to see to my own."

"Are you simply a little fool? Or is your defiance of my wishes something more?"

She lifted her head like a queen. "I know not what you mean, sir. The call went out for help, and I simply answered it. Now if you'll excuse me…"

She started to step down, and was forced to catch her breath as his big arms came around her waist, lifting her as though she weighed no more than a wee child. Again she felt the most amazing flutter around her heart at the mere touch of him.

She found it difficult to speak over the constriction in her throat. "Thank you, sir."

He set her on her feet and studied her with a growing frown. How pretty she looked, all fresh-faced and refreshed from her night at the inn. Not that he had time to enjoy the sight. He had more pressing issues than this annoying woman who called herself a witch.

"A warning, my lady. You might refrain from trying another of your spells, lest you find yourself on a distant mountain top, or swimming in a strange loch."

Though there wasn't even the hint of laughter in his eyes, she knew that he was having fun with her.

"You'd best mind your tongue, sir, or I might be tempted to try one of my spells on you."

"I believe you already have. How else to explain why I didn't have you banished the moment I saw you?"

He turned away and stalked off to join the workers, leaving her to stare after him.

One of the women from the village called out to him, "With your permission, we would like to take the tapestries back to the village, to see if they can be mended."

"Aye." Andrew nodded. "Though I'm not certain any can be salvaged."

"Some are badly burned. But others are merely charred. Most of our women are deft with needle and thread, and we wish to do what we can to restore the castle to its former beauty."

"That's kind of you, Mistress. I am most grateful."

Just as the woman walked away, one of the men summoned him to settle a dispute over the best way to remove one of the larger timbers.

As Andrew joined him, Gwenellen followed the women inside the castle which, she learned, was composed of two buildings; one an ancient abbey, which was largely unused; the other a newer addition built within the past hundred years to serve as both home and fortress.

Soon she was caught up in the scrubbing and polishing, sweeping and cleaning. Sleeping chambers on the upper level were stripped of their sooty linens and window coverings and scrubbed to a high shine before fresh rushes were added to the floors. In a corner of the walled garden, village lasses were busy hanging the wash that fluttered in the breeze.

So many people, Gwenellen thought. And all of them working toward a common goal. She found the work oddly satisfying, and was soon laughing and chatting with the others.

In the great hall charred timbers were hauled away, while in the nearby forest new ones were cut and hewn before being loaded onto wagons. Along with the timbers, the village men loaded several stags that had been brought down by hunters' arrows.

While crofters planed and shaped the giant timbers, and struggled to set them into place, the stags roasted over several fire pits.

By the time evening shadows began to gather, the rooms of the abbey were warmed by fires burning on the giant hearths. The fragrance of bread baking and meat roasting perfumed the air.

Andrew clapped his hands for silence. "My friends. You have labored long and hard. Before you return to your homes, you must allow me to thank you. The women have prepared a feast. And Duncan has unearthed several casks of fine ale."

With shouts and cheering the men and women eagerly followed him into the great hall and settled themselves at long tables, while the younger lasses hurried about serving food and ale.

Andrew disdained the lone head table, choosing instead to sit at a table in the middle of the room, surrounded by the people who had worked alongside him throughout the long day.

It occurred to Gwenellen that even without any visible sign, it was apparent that Andrew Ross was a leader among these people. Despite the anger that simmered just beneath the surface, and the soot that once more stained his clothes, as well as the raw and blistered hands from his painful labors this day, there was about him a manner, a bearing, that set him apart as a man others would respect.

Duncan stood and lifted his goblet, waiting until the others grew silent. "We are truly sorry for your loss, Andrew. Your father was a fine man, and a fair one." The old man glanced around at his friends and neighbors. "Many of us lost loved ones who had attended your family, and we grieve along with you. We have spoken among ourselves, and have agreed to pledge to you this night our loyalty and our weapons. With the old laird gone, we declare you laird of the Ross clan. When you are ready to move against Fergus Logan and his hated clan, we will join you in seeking justice."

The men got to their feet, adding their voices to Duncan's before emptying their goblets.

Gwenellen saw the look that came into Andrew's

eyes. A dark look that no amount of cheering would dispel.

It would appear that the mere mention of his enemy had his blood hot for revenge. It was obvious that the laird of Ross Abbey would not be satisfied until those who had committed their foul deeds were made to pay.

She thought about the words his father had spoken from his grave, and realized her dilemma. If she were to admit that she could speak with the dead, there would be many in this world who would condemn her as evil. Yet how could she convince Andrew of his father's wishes without revealing her gift?

Agitated, she slipped away from the great hall and made her way along the empty corridors until she found herself in the small, walled garden littered with fresh graves.

At once the voices assaulted her from all sides.

"Please, my lady, inform my wife and children that I watch over them still."

"A moment, my lady. I have a brother in the village who isn't doing his duty towards my granddaughter. You must remind him that she needs him to look after her, now more than ever."

"Hold, lass." An old man's voice, as soft as a whisper in the wind, stopped her.

Recognizing it, Gwenellen paused.

"Ye must tell Andrew to accept the decree of his people and accept the title of laird. But he must not

*march against Fergus Logan. It is important that he
remain here, close to those who look to him for guidance and protection.''*

Gwenellen dropped to her knees beside the mound
of dirt where a handsome man sat on the boulder that
marked the grave. Gone were the hideous wounds
and bloody flesh she'd seen on the lifeless body of
Andrew's father. This man looked years younger,
and more like Andrew's brother than his father. Still,
she recognized him at once.

"You've changed."

"Have I?" He stroked his chin. Smiled. *"Age is
something only experienced in your world, lass. Now
I'll be eternally young and strong."* His voice lowered with passion. *"Now, about my son. Ye must convince him to accept his role as leader and remain
here, rather than going off with some foolish notion
of vengeance burning like a fever in his blood.''*

"It isn't only vengeance that drives him. He feels
he must rescue your wife."

"The lovely Sabrina." Something in his tone
changed. *"Rest assured. She'll not be harmed.''*

"How do you know?"

His eyes narrowed. *"I know.''*

"How can I tell him so without appearing mad?"

*"What does it matter how ye look to him? It only
matters that he believes ye.''*

"But how am I to make him believe? He's too

filled with anger and bitterness to listen. Besides, he believes me a charlatan.''

"Then tell him the truth."

"That I can see you? Hear you?''

"Aye. What's wrong with that?"

"You know what's wrong. He can't see you, and he's your own son.''

"Ye're the one with the gift, lass. What good is it if ye can't use it for those who most need it?"

His question left her without an argument. She pondered it a moment, then nodded. "Aye. What good, indeed?''

There was a long moment of silence. *"Ye'll tell him?"*

She nodded. "I will. And I'll find a way to make him believe me.''

"That's my lass." The old man patted her hand and she felt a cool, damp sheen to her flesh, as though brushed by a mist.

She looked over. "I know not your name.''

"Morgan Ross, lass. I was named for my great grandfather, who was said to come from the sea."

"And I am Gwenellen Drummond.''

"Aye. I know ye'r father, lass. He was here to welcome me when I slipped over to the other side."

"He was?'' Her tone softened. "He passed before I was born, but we've had many fine visits.''

"Aye, lass. When I told him I couldna' rest until I set my son on the right course, he told me not to

worry, for he was sending me someone special. Ye mustn'a fail me, Gwenellen Drummond.''

"I'll do my best, Morgan Ross."

"What are you doing out here?" A voice, sharp with anger and suspicion, sounded directly behind Gwenellen, causing her to freeze.

A hand closed roughly on her shoulder. "Who the devil are you talking to?"

She turned to see the hilt of a knife glinting in Andrew's hand, and the dark light of fury in his narrowed gaze.

"It's as I suspected. You conspire with my enemies. Tell me quickly, woman, who you are meeting under cover of darkness." He lifted his hand in a menacing gesture. "Before I cut out your lying heart."

Chapter Five

Gwenellen shrank back, stung by his anger. "I would never betray you to your enemies."

"You don't deny that you were talking to someone when I walked up?"

"Aye. I was." She nodded toward the vision seated on the boulder. "Your father."

He followed her gaze, then swung back, anger and suspicion visible in his narrowed eyes. "Don't make sport of me, woman. I've neither time nor patience for your foolishness."

Remembering her promise to his father, she put aside her fear and lifted her head, returning his look. "Your father has a message for you, my lord. And because he can't speak to you directly, he must speak through me."

He gave a hiss of impatience and tightened his grasp on the handle of the knife. "Don't call me by the title lord. I've no intention of accepting such an honor, for I was trained as a warrior, not a noble. After seeing the way the nobles behave at Court, I've no taste for such a life.''

Gwenellen took a deep breath. ''Your father asks that you accept the will of your people. Further, he desires that you remain here, rather than going off to confront your enemies.''

''He does, does he? And what says he of his wife who is being held captive?''

''He claims she will not be harmed by your enemies.''

He fixed her with a fearsome look. ''At least on that we can agree.'' He studied her, his mouth a taut line of anger. ''You will leave now, woman, and join those who go about their evil deeds. If you dare to show your face to me again, you'll taste the justice of Andrew Ross.''

As he started away she spoke quickly, the words tumbling from her lips. ''Your father told me his name is Morgan.''

Andrew turned back. ''You're a clever woman. I see you spent your time here in my castle well enough, learning all you could about my family.''

''I could have. Instead, I spent my time working alongside the others.'' And had the fresh blisters to prove it, she thought bitterly. ''I can't make you believe me, my lord. Not when your heart is closed to the truth. But I gave your father my word that I would try. He asks but two things of you. That you accept the will of your people, and that you do not ride to the fortress of your enemy. You can heed his words from beyond this world, or you can deny them, as you deny me.'' Gwenellen glanced over and saw his father's face etched in sadness, beginning to blur and fade before it disappeared completely.

She had failed. Once again.

Awash in disappointment, she started to sweep past this man who had aroused an entirely new emotion inside her. Anger. It ran hot and swift through her veins. Never before had she known this feeling, and she didn't much care for it.

''Where do you think you're going, woman?''

''I'll return to the village with the others, and leave you to your grief and misery, since you've made it abundantly clear that you have no use for me here.''

''A pity you tarried here so long. The villagers have all gone.''

''Gone?'' Her eyes widened. ''But how am I to return to the village tavern?''

His tone was mocking. ''Perhaps one of those spells you boast of will carry you off.''

He strode past her and started toward the castle, leaving her staring after him.

At the door he paused, then turned. ''Despite my misgivings about you, it goes against everything I've been taught to leave you alone in the chill night air. I feel obliged to offer you the shelter of my home.''

Relieved, she stepped toward him.

As she moved past him he put a hand to her arm. His voice was low with feeling. "But only for the night. On the morrow I'll see you returned to the village, and from there to your kingdom. And this time, you'll not defy me as you did today."

"Defy you? You speak as though you were laird of the land."

He shot her an angry look. "If I choose the title, you'd best fear my wrath, woman, for here in the Highlands, the laird's word is law. If I command my men to kill you, it will be done without question."

Gwenellen stiffened her spine and followed him up the stairs, all the while considering his words, for she knew they were true.

Andrew opened a set of doors and led the way into one of the sleeping chambers. He had deliberately chosen the one farthest from his own.

Seeing that the fire had burned low he turned away. "I'll fetch enough wood to get you through the night, and some fresh water."

When he was gone Gwenellen looked around. The village women had done a thorough job. In the sleeping chamber a pallet had been covered with fresh linens and fur throws. On a night stand stood a basin and pitcher, as well as several linen towels.

Shivering, Gwenellen wondered how long it would take Andrew to fetch logs from the great hall below. How much simpler it would be to work a spell.

What was the harm in trying?

She walked closer and extended her arms. Closing her eyes she began to chant the ancient words.

Still simmering with anger, Andrew welcomed the chance to do something physical. He lifted an armful of logs that would stagger most men and started up the stairs.

This annoying little female had spoiled whatever momentary happiness lingered from the feast with the villagers. Such good people. They had spent the day laboring on his behalf, and had seemed genuinely sorry for his loss. And why not? Though he and his father had argued bitterly, Morgan Ross had been a good and fair man, sharing his bounty with his friends and neighbors, and all who were in need. He'd raised his only son to do the same. The two had been inseparable until Sabrina. Then everything between father and son had changed.

Sabrina. The very thought of his father's wife had temper flaring. Perhaps she was one more reason why he'd refused the title of laird of his people. Being laird separated a man from his people. Set him apart, and above. No man should be above another. Especially a father over his son.

Andrew stepped into the sitting parlor and paused on the threshold. From within the sleeping chamber came the sound of Gwenellen's chanting. Though the words were unknown to him, he couldn't help but be touched by the sound of that soft, breathy voice. It had an other-world quality that never failed to touch some chord deep inside him.

The firewood was forgotten as he crossed the room and paused in the doorway. He was riveted to the spot at the sight of her, arms extended, eyes closed, that glorious spill of golden curls tumbling below her waist.

Suddenly the chanting ceased, and he heard her words clearly.

"Hear me, lest you taste my ire. I call to this hearth a breath of fire."

There was a sound, as though of a great wind, that set her skirts fluttering around her ankles and lifted her hair, sending it dancing madly around her shoulders.

In the doorway Andrew watched in stunned fascination. His first thought was that he'd greatly misjudged this woman, for only a true witch could command the elements in such a manner.

With a deafening roar a great gust of wind came rushing down the chimney, swirling soot and ash in its path. Seeing it rolling over the room in a huge black wave, Andrew fell to the floor and waited for it to pass overhead.

Gwenellen wasn't as fortunate. Still standing, arms extended, she was battered and buffeted by the wave. By the time it passed, she was bent double, coughing and retching.

Andrew tossed aside the firewood and rushed to

her side. He caught her by the arms and helped her to her feet. "My lady. Speak to me. Are you harmed?"

When she lifted her face, she could hardly speak over the dust in her throat.

Andrew struggled not to laugh at the sight of her. Her face and arms, her hair, her gown, were all coated with soot and ash. The only thing left to see were the whites of her eyes. And those were flashing in outrage and growing temper.

"I'm unharmed. Leave me."

Instead of doing as she asked he walked to the night table and filled the basin with water. Moistening a linen square he turned and began to wipe the soot from her face.

"I can do that for myself." Humiliation stung her cheeks and roughened her tone as she snatched the cloth from his hand.

He watched as she scrubbed her face with more force than necessary.

All the while he peered at her closely. "You were attempting to light a fire on the hearth with one of your spells?"

She held her silence.

Taking pity on her he relented. "Perhaps I misjudged you, my lady. It would appear that you do fancy yourself a witch."

"Fancy myself? I'm not a witch. I'm a fool." She turned away, unable to bear his studied looks and

forced kindness. "If either of my sisters had attempted that spell, these chambers would be warm
and cozy. Instead…" She looked around, horrified
at the soot and ash that covered the floor, the pallet,
the walls. "Instead, I've ruined everything the village
women worked so hard to achieve this day."

He touched a hand to her shoulder. "It doesn't
matter, my lady."

"But it does." She pulled free of his touch and
forced herself to meet his eyes. "Don't you see? I
can't do any of the things the rest of my family can
do with ease. And the one thing I can do is of no
importance to anyone, because nobody would ever
believe that I can actually speak with the dead."

"Is it so important that others believe?"

She clutched the linen square in her fist. "How
can I convey the messages from the other side if no
one believes in the messenger?"

He thought about that before nodding. "I suppose
that would be a problem. Very well." He bent and
picked up the logs, then turned toward the doorway.
"You will tell me again what my father said."

Her head came up sharply. "You'll listen?"

"Aye. But first I must find you another chamber,
and something to wear until your clothes have been
cleaned."

Confused, Gwenellen danced along behind him,
struggling to keep up with his hurried footsteps.

"You mean I'm welcome to stay the night? You're not just tolerating me out of a sense of duty?"

He bit back the grin that was curling the corners of his mouth. If she knew how she looked, her hair and face and garments blackened with soot, she'd be even more embarrassed than she was by her failed spell.

He led her down the hallway toward the chambers beside his, consoling himself that it was only for a few more hours. How much could go wrong in a single night?

"Here you are, my lady." He dropped several logs on the fire in the sitting parlor, then carried the rest to the sleeping chambers beyond.

Gwenellen looked around and realized that this suite of rooms was even more elegant than the first. The chaise positioned in front of the fireplace had been draped with furs for comfort. On a side table was a decanter of ale and several goblets. Judging by the freshly-washed garments hanging on pegs along one wall, this had once belonged to the old laird's wife, the mistress of Ross Abbey.

When the fire was blazing, Andrew stood and wiped his hands on his tunic before turning to her. "I'll give you time to refresh yourself. You may choose whatever garments suit you. Then, if you'd like, I'll return and you can tell me again about your…visit with my father."

"Thank you." Subdued, Gwenellen waited until

he'd taken his leave before stripping off her clothes and filling a basin with water. After scrubbing herself clean, she carefully washed her hair and then her gown and undergarments, hanging them on pegs to dry.

She chose a simple white nightshirt with low, rounded neckline and long tapered sleeves, and over that a robe of cut velvet the color of claret. From the way they fit her, it was obvious that the old laird's wife had been reed-slender. A great deal of care had gone into the weaving of the garments, revealing a woman of obvious wealth and taste.

After dressing, Gwenellen twisted her damp hair into one fat braid which spilled over her breast.

After the exhausting day she'd put in, she ought to be tired. But the thought of relaying the truth to Andrew about his father had her twitching with excitement. Perhaps, finally, she would be able to use her gift for some good.

The knock on her door had her hurrying to the sitting parlor.

''Enter, my lord.''

Andrew moved past her. He had removed his tunic and hose and wore only the plaid, which he'd tossed over one bare shoulder.

She remembered the first time she'd seen a Highland laird dressed in such a fashion. It was when her sister Allegra had returned to the Mystical Kingdom with her beloved abductor, Merrick. At first sight he'd seemed a giant and a barbarian. But beneath that stern facade her sister had uncovered a tender, loving heart.

Gwenellen doubted there would be either tenderness or love in this stern warrior. Not that she cared. All she wanted to do was carry out her mission for those in that other world, so that she could return with pride to her own.

Andrew filled two goblets with ale and handed one to her before tilting his head back and taking a long drink. Then he strode to the fireplace and rested his arm along the mantel, trying not to stare.

He'd had quite a jolt when he'd first seen Gwenellen in Sabrina's regal clothing. This woman, however, was too much of an imp to look like anything that even faintly resembled royalty. Still, something about this simple female stirred him in a way he resented. Even her bare toes, peeking out from beneath the hem of her nightdress, held his gaze longer than he would have preferred.

"Now, my lady, tell me everything my father said to you."

She sipped the ale and settled herself on the chaise. "There is little enough to tell. Your father first called out to me when you found him in the rubble, though at first I wasn't certain what I was hearing."

"Because you'd never before spoken to the dead?"

"I've spoken to my father for all my life." Seeing

the arch of his brow she explained. "My father died before I was born. But throughout my lifetime I've often seen him and spoken with him. Gram said it was one of my greatest gifts, but I never understood. You see, there were no others in the Mystical Kingdom who had passed to that other side."

She'd managed to scrub away all the soot and ash and now looked, to his eye, as fresh and colorful as a rainbow. It was difficult to concentrate on her word when he was so affected by her looks, but he was determined. "So you heard my father calling to you."

She nodded. "And the others."

"Others?" His lips curved in a smile. He'd give her this much. She was a grand weaver of tales. "What others?"

"There was a woman named Melvina, who told me she was a niece to Mistress MacIntosh. She was sorry about helping herself to a kettle of stew, and then blaming it on one of the serving wenches, who lost her employment. And a man named Roland, who claims his brother Shepard is not taking care of a grandchild left behind. And a young scullery wench, Charity, who—"

"Hold." Andrew lifted his hand to stop her, then took a moment to drain his tankard. Refilling it, he walked closer, his eyes narrowed on her. "Are these more tales you heard while working with the villagers?"

"It's as I told you. I heard it from those who have passed to the other side. Before they can find peace, they must settle any debts they left behind."

"Debts." He blinked. "And they hope you will help them clear their debts?"

"Aye." She seemed so honest. So direct. And, in truth, he'd heard of the servant who'd been dismissed from Duncan's tavern for stealing a kettle of stew, though she'd protested her innocence. As for the others, they had all worked here in the castle. Could it be…?

"And my father?" He dropped to his knees before her, his eyes intent upon hers. "Tell me again everything my father said."

She repeated everything she could recall from their conversation. When she finished, she found herself wondering if he believed her. It was impossible to tell from the look in those icy eyes, but at least he had listened in respectful silence.

"Oh." She smiled, remembering. "Your father told me one other thing. He said he'd been named for his grandfather, who was said to come from the sea."

Andrew scrambled to his feet, his hand fisted tightly around the tankard. "It was something my father was most proud of." He seemed to be talking to himself. "He'd thought to name me after his grandfather, as well, but had been convinced by my mother to honor her father instead."

Abruptly he looked over at her. "Go to sleep now, my lady." He drained his ale and set the tankard on the side table, keeping his gaze averted. "I'll think on all you've told me."

It wasn't what she'd hoped for, but at least the sarcasm was gone from his tone.

As he started from the room, he had a quick impression of the soot and ash littering the chambers down the hall. He turned, the merest hint of a smile in his eyes. "Before retiring I would ask a favor, my lady."

"Aye." She turned to him with a hopeful look.

"If you would, promise me you'll attempt no spells until this night is over."

Before she could respond he was gone, leaving her feeling oddly deflated. Not only did he not believe her, but he also didn't trust her.

And why should he? she thought with a wave of revulsion. She couldn't even trust herself to complete the simplest spell.

She stormed off to bed, eager to have this night behind her. She had done as his father had requested. She had conveyed his words from that other place.

On the morrow she would return to the Mystical Kingdom. And there she would remain, so that the rest of the world would never know of her shameful failure.

Chapter Six

Andrew paced in front of the fire in his chambers, playing back everything in his mind.

Was he a fool to even consider believing this woman? She spoke of the dead and their debts as though she were speaking of the logic of fish in the loch, birds in the sky. But he'd seen fish swim and birds fly. He'd never seen walking, talking dead, though he'd heard of such things, but always by wild-eyed crones speaking in whispers, as though afraid to be overheard by those who might call their bluff.

If his father had things to say, why did he speak to a stranger instead of to the son who loved him?

Perhaps because the son wouldn't listen.

The thought startled him. But the more he chewed on it, the more he knew it to be true. Would he have listened to the whisperings of his heart? Or would he simply allow the pain of his grief to crowd out all other thoughts from his mind?

Wasn't that what he'd been doing since returning home? Hadn't his every thought been about avenging the death of his father? Not only because it was his duty, but because he felt responsible. If he hadn't argued and left when he did, none of this would have happened. And now he could never take back the things he'd said in anger.

Still, what the woman claimed to have heard made no sense to him. He was a warrior. Why would his father want him to remain here, dwelling in comfort in a castle, while allowing his enemies to go unpunished? Especially since those same enemies were holding an innocent woman captive?

Unless his father knew something he didn't.

He stalked to the balcony of his room and stared down at the land below, bathed in darkness. He loved this place as he loved no other. Even the queen's luxurious appointments at Holyroodhouse in Edinburgh hadn't been enough to tempt him to stay away. There were some who found life at the palace heady stuff indeed. Many of his warriors had been delighted at the assignment to remain in Edinburgh and guard the queen. As for him, he much preferred the slower pace of life in his beloved Highlands. He loved every glen and fall and craggy hilltop. Loved the rushing water in springtime, and the dusting of snow in winter. Best of all he loved the summer sunshine, and meadows abloom with heather.

The woman, Gwenellen, reminded him of summer. There was a brightness, a shiny newness about her unlike any other woman he'd ever known. That mane of golden hair looked like liquid sunshine. And that bright smile that found its way even into her eyes, was dazzling, like sunlight reflecting off the clear surface of a loch.

Was she truly a witch? Or had she been sent by his enemies to play with his mind?

If a witch, she was a poor enough one. That little scene with the fire was proof enough that she needed a great deal more time before she could claim supernatural powers. Just thinking about it had him grinning. Soot and ash all the way to her eyebrows. And the look on her face when she realized her spell had gone awry. By heaven she was a delight to watch.

Still, for all her confusion, she'd accurately described his father and some of the servants who had perished with him.

Perhaps on the morrow he would ask her to seek out his father for answers to the questions that were burning holes in his mind.

What would it hurt to keep her around for another day? Aye, and then he would send her back to her Mystical Kingdom, if indeed such a place existed.

He dropped down onto his pallet and pressed a

hand to his eyes, wishing he could still the thoughts that flitted through his mind. Thoughts of the heated exchange between him and his father before he'd left, vowing never to return. Thoughts of barbarians storming the gates of Ross Abbey, cutting down all in their path. Of his father, without the aid and comfort of his only son as he lay dying.

It was a scene that burned like a fire deep in his brain, denying him the peace he sought.

Gwenellen awoke and lay a moment, struggling to recall where she was. There had been so many changes in her young life in the past few days. And all of them confusing.

She opened her eyes to see sunlight spilling across the balcony and into her chambers. Stretching, she sat up and listened to the chatter of birds as she washed. Finding her gown dry she slipped it on and carefully hung her borrowed nightdress and robe on a peg before straightening her pallet.

When she stepped from her chambers she inhaled the wonderful perfume of meat roasting. Following the scent, she made her way below stairs to the refectory where she found Andrew turning several birds on a spit over a blazing fire.

''Good morrow.'' He'd vowed upon awakening to bury his anger and make an attempt to be civil. He looked over and felt a jolt at the sight of her. The gown was simple enough, as were the kid boots, though he much preferred seeing her bare feet.

"Good morrow. You have no one to cook for you?"

"I'm a warrior. I learned long ago to care for my own needs while away from home. Between battles I can cook enough to keep body and soul together. And I can even mend my tunic, if necessary."

"You can ply a needle?" She picked up a knife and began slicing a loaf of bread left over from their evening feast.

"I can." He removed a bird and placed it on a platter before cutting it neatly in two. "And how about you, my lady? Have you been schooled in the womanly arts?"

He saw the way she wrinkled her nose. Such a cute, turned-up little nose. If he looked closely, he could spot a sprinkling of freckles parading across the bridge of it, and spilling over onto her cheeks.

"My sisters and I are the despair of our mother, who can weave and sew anything, and old Bessie, who cooks like an angel."

"What can you and your sisters do?" He placed half of the bird in front of her before taking a seat across the scarred wooden table.

She nibbled the bread. "Allegra is a healer. There is no wound she cannot heal. Kylia can look into a man's eyes and see what is in his heart. And I..." She looked away.

"You can speak to the dead."

Her head came up sharply. "Do you believe that, or are you now having fun with me?"

He studied the challenge in her eyes and gave a slight nod of his head. "I've had time to think about the things you told me. I'd like you to ask my father some questions."

"Gladly." Her food was forgotten as her mood suddenly brightened. "What questions?"

"I need to know why he wishes me to remain here instead of storming the castle of Fergus Logan to rescue the lady Sabrina."

Gwenellen nodded. "Would you like me to ask him now?"

He glanced at her food. "I think you'd be wise to eat first, my lady. If you summon those from the other world the way you cast your spells, it could be some time before you eat again."

He saw the flush on her cheeks as she ducked her head. At once he felt remorse for having reminded her of her failures.

"While we eat, you can tell me more about your Mystical Kingdom. What do you do for pleasure, besides hunt berries?"

She picked at the fowl. "I have my horse, Starlight."

"An odd name. Do you ride it a great distance?"

"We fly among the stars."

"You...fly?"

She dimpled. "Starlight is a winged horse. There are two others. Sunlight belongs to Allegra, and Moonlight is Kylia's steed."

"And the three of you...fly?"

"Sometimes the fairies accompany us, but they prefer not to get lost in the clouds, so they often stay in the treetops."

"Fairies. Winged horses. And of course, your troll."

"He isn't my troll. Jeremy is just..." She searched for a word. "He's just Jeremy."

"How did your family come to be in the Mystical Kingdom?"

"We fled our home in the Highlands when we were warned that we might be put into Tolbooth Prison for plying our craft."

"Witchcraft."

She ducked her head. "It happened because my sister Allegra healed a lad who had drowned."

"Healed him? You mean she brought him back from the dead?"

Gwenellen smiled. "He wasn't truly dead. She could hear him calling out, though his voice was heard only by Allegra. Her tender heart was touched by the grief of his poor mother. So Allegra laid her hands upon him and brought him back. But there were many in the crowd who were complaining about what they thought to be the devil's work. So that night, we fled to the home of our ancestors, and we've remained there since.''

"How did your father feel about marrying a witch?''

Gwenellen's smile deepened. ''Theirs was a love match. Though he didn't understand my mother's gifts, he loved her enough to accept her as she is. My grandmother says such love is pre-ordained. It is written in the stars, and can neither be denied nor extinguished. Even after death, it survives through all ages.''

She sat back, her food forgotten. ''I miss them. And my home.''

Andrew heard the wistfulness in her tone and understood. Hadn't it been the same for him in Edinburgh? Despite the luxury of court, he'd been eager to return to his rugged Highlands.

Gwenellen pushed away from the table. ''If you don't mind, I believe I'll go out to the garden now and ask your father the questions you've posed.''

Andrew watched her walk away, then pushed aside his own food, his appetite suddenly gone.

Fairies. Winged horses. Trolls. What sort of fool did she take him for? Still, there was no denying the look that came into her eyes when she spoke about her home. What a treat it would be to see such a place, if it truly existed.

He got to his feet and hurried out of the room, eager to catch up with her. He wouldn't miss this for the world.

"Good morrow, my lord Morgan." Gwenellen was pleased to see Andrew's father sitting on the boulder atop his grave.

"Good morrow, lass. I'm proud of ye. It isn't easy getting past my son's anger. But ye're getting to him, just as ye'r father promised." Blue eyes twinkled with pleasure. *"He's beginning to believe."*

"He's willing to try. But you must give me something more, my lord Morgan. Something that will chase away any lingering doubts."

"Something more, eh, lass?" The older man stretched out his long legs and leaned back on the boulder, deep in thought. A slow smile spread across his face, and Gwenellen was reminded of Andrew. There were times when he looked at her, that she felt as though he were trying not to laugh.

"Sit here, lass." He indicated the grass beside his grave.

As Gwenellen settled herself, he crossed his ankles. *"I'll tell you a tale from Andrew's childhood, that nobody else knows."* He took his time, going back in his mind. *"Andrew's mother had a fondness for roses. All summer, she carefully tended her garden, nurturing each tiny plant. But though she did everything possible, they never produced flowers. Occasionally there would be a few buds, but alas they never lasted long enough to bloom. They would simply wither and die on the vine. The year Andrew was four, my wife Laurel persuaded one of the royal gardeners to visit our keep. He spent several weeks here, instructing Laurel and our gardeners on the proper way to grow roses. By the time he left, the plants had produced dozens of promising buds. Laurel was in a state of high excitement, for it would be the first time her beloved roses would bloom.''*

Gwenellen watched his eyes sparkle with humor. He was thoroughly enjoying himself as he recalled the event.

''Now, ye should know that Andrew adored his mother, and her excitement conveyed itself to him. Each morning, when Laurel walked the garden, the lad would skip along beside her, his excitement equal to hers. The day the first of the roses finally bloomed, she bent to inhale the wonderful perfume of each one, and spent the rest of the afternoon telling all who would listen about the beauty of her flowers. The next morning she could hardly wait to hurry to the garden to admire her treasure. Imagine her horror when she found every single bloom gone. All that remained were bare stems.''

Gwenellen was so caught up in the story, she looked as horrified as Laurel must have looked on that day. ''Who would do such a cruel thing, my lord Morgan?''

''Who indeed?'' He sat forward, hands on his

knees. *"Poor Laurel paced the floor of her chambers, imagining a score of ways to punish the rogue who had robbed her of her greatest pleasure. Just then young Andrew came rushing into her room, his little arms filled with rose petals. He'd awakened early just to go to the garden so that he could surprise his mother with the fragrance she loved. Of course, at that tender age, he had no idea what he'd done. His tender fingers were bloody from the prick of thorns, but his smile was so radiant, how could his mother resist his offering?"*

"What did she do with the rose petals?"

"What any mother would, I suppose. She lifted the petals to her face and breathed in their perfume, then she tossed them across the bed and invited Andrew to roll in them with her." He gave a roar of laughter. *"That's how I found them. Giggling together and rolling in rose petals."* His smile faded. *"Years later, when Laurel lay dying, she told me it was one of her fondest memories."*

Gwenellen felt tears burn the back of her lids and had to blink quickly. "Thank you for sharing that tale, my lord Morgan. I believe it will convince Andrew of the truth of what I say. Now I must ask you the question he has given me. Why must he remain here, instead of rescuing your bride from the clutches of your enemy?"

He was already shaking his head. *"To do so would be to invite disaster, for Fergus Logan is expecting*

Andrew to do just that. Instead, he must confound
his enemy by doing that which he wouldn't expect.''

"And the Lady Sabrina?"

His smile faded. *"Ye may tell Andrew that he was
right and I was wrong.''*

"That's all?"

"Aye. 'Tis all I have to say at this time."

"But why? Doesn't your son deserve to know all
that you do, my lord?"

"Not if such knowledge will destroy him."

"I don't understand."

He leaned forward and took her hands in his. As
before, she felt the brush of something cool and
damp against her flesh. *"It isn't necessary that ye
understand, lass. Only that ye tell Andrew what I've
told ye."*

She heard the footfall behind her and looked over
to see Andrew standing very still, watching her with
an unfathomable look. The image of his father began
to blur, then faded from sight.

She got to her feet and shook down her skirts. As
she started toward him she couldn't help smiling at
the image of a wee lad beaming with pleasure as he
offered up his surprise to the mother he adored.
Though it was at odds with this angry warrior who
now stood before her, it was an image she would not
soon forget.

Chapter Seven

"**Y**ou spoke with him?" Andrew had stood in the shadows, hearing her voice, soft and low, and the long silences that could only mean she was listening to someone, or something.

Voices in her head?

"Aye. Your father was here. And looking much as you look now."

That fact caught him by surprise. Though it was true that many might still consider Morgan Ross a handsome, dashing warrior, Andrew could remember only the father with whom he'd bitterly argued in their last confrontation. It was impossible to imagine him young and virile, now that death had claimed him.

Or was this just her overactive imagination?

He glanced toward the fresh mound of earth where his father's body now lay. Seeing the direction of his glance, she steered him toward the door of the castle, knowing it was best for him to leave this place that still caused him such pain. At her prodding, Andrew reluctantly moved along beside her.

Once inside he paused beside the great stairway. "Did my father answer my question? Did he tell you why I should remain here in the comfort of my own home instead of rescuing Sabrina?"

"Aye. He said that is what your enemy anticipates. And so you must do the unexpected and remain here."

"And bide my time? He must know that goes against everything I believe in. I'm a warrior." Andrew's eyes narrowed. "Did he tell you anything else?"

"Only that you were right about Lady Sabrina and he was wrong."

For a moment he looked thunderstruck. "You're certain those were his words?"

"Aye."

"What else did he say?"

"Nothing more. And when I asked why, he explained that to say more would destroy you."

Andrew snagged her wrist. "And I say it is the not knowing that will destroy me. If you were who you claimed to be, you would have demanded more. Unless, of course, you were sent here by my enemies to further confound me." He dragged her close, his eyes fixed on hers with a look that had her heart leaping to her throat. There was about him the same fierce look that she'd first encountered. He touched a hand to the jeweled hilt of a knife at his waist. "Tell me why I should not kill you, woman."

"Because I am not your enemy."

"Aye. You claim to be merely a poor, befuddled soul whose simplest spells go awry, yet you boast that you can speak with the dead. This time, woman, you will prove it to me beyond a doubt, or you'll pay with your life."

She tried to draw away but he held her fast.

Though her heart was pounding in her chest, she lifted her chin defiantly. "I knew this would be your reaction. I was certain you would be reluctant to believe me. I asked for something that would open your heart and mind. Your father told me about an incident when you were very small."

"You'll tell me of this…imaginary childhood incident, woman. And if it is something I can't vividly recall, have no doubt that your blood will be on my hands."

Her voice trembled as she relayed the tale that had been told to her. When she finished, she could tell, from the stunned look in his eyes, that he not only remembered, but had been deeply moved by the retelling of it.

He uncurled his fingers from around her wrist and took a step back, all the while staring into her eyes without a word.

The silence stretched between them for so long,

she finally touched a hand to his, only to have him jerk back.

His voice was low with feeling. ''You could not have learned this from anyone except my father.''

Relief flooded through her. She stood very still, giving him the time he needed to absorb this knowledge and accept the implications of it.

He took in a long, deep breath. His tone softened. ''Forgive me for doubting you, my lady. I've never before known anyone who could talk to those on the other side.''

''Nor have I ever had the privilege, except with my father, until now.''

His voice nearly trembled with emotion. ''Now that I know you can do what you claim, I would beg a favor of you.''

Startled, she could do nothing more than nod. ''Name it.''

''Will you remain at Ross Abbey, at least for a while longer? For there is much I wish to ask my father.''

She let out a quiet breath, too surprised to speak. It would seem that he was now ready to accept what he could not understand. If he was not fully convinced, at least he was willing to believe in her power, meager though it might be.

Mistaking her silence for disapproval he quickly added, ''I realize that life here is far from what you're accustomed to in your kingdom. From what you've described, it will never be the paradise you left behind. But if you'll give me some time, I'll inquire in the village for servants. Though Ross Abbey will never take the place of your home, I'll do all in my power to make it as comfortable for you as possible, if you'll agree to remain.''

She nodded. "I will stay."

He was already shaking his head. "Please don't be quick to refuse for I know...." He stopped. Closed his mouth. Opened it again. "You'll stay?"

"I will. For as long as you need me."

He caught her hands in his and bowed over them. "Thank you, my lady."

"There is one thing, though. I must send a missive to my family letting them know that I'm safe."

He nodded. "If you but tell me how, I'll see to it."

She thought a moment. "Is there a falconer in the village?"

"There is."

She smiled. "If you would have him send the falcon heavenward with my missive, it will reach the Mystical Kingdom."

He nodded. "It will be done this very day. I am most humbly grateful, my lady, for I know this can't be an easy decision for you."

As he brushed his lips over the back of her hands he had a quick recollection of the last time he'd kissed her. Looking up he could see the color rising to her cheeks and knew that she was remembering it, too.

His first thought was to kiss her full on the mouth. He'd never forgotten her sweet taste. It had left him oddly hungry for more. Still, if he were to follow his instincts and kiss her, he might frighten her away. And though it galled him to admit it, he needed this odd little creature. She was, to him, a calm port in a sea swirling with storms of lies and deceit.

He lowered her hands, released them, and took a step back. "There is more to the tale my father told you."

"More?"

"Aye. That same day my mother gave me this dirk." Again he touched the jeweled hilt that winked in the sunlight. "It belonged to my mother's father, and she told me that he had been a most kind and generous laird of his clan. She believed that, as the son of a laird, and the grandson of two, I would one day be a leader of my people." His voice roughened. "This means much to me, because the one who gave it to me is always close in my heart. It has remained on my person since the day she gave it to me." With his hand on the hilt he added, "I go now to the village, for I must tell the people that I accept the title they have thrust upon me."

"That will make your father and mother most happy, my lord."

He tried not to flinch at her use of that title. It

would take a great deal of time to adjust his thinking of himself as laird of his clan instead of merely a warrior. "Is there anything I might bring you?"

She shook her head. "I require nothing."

She could feel him studying her before he turned away. After opening the door he turned back. A hint of a smile touched his lips. "You won't try any of your...spells while I'm gone?"

She'd just begun to relax. Now the awkwardness was back. "Have no fear, my lord. I wouldn't want to risk destroying your castle after all the work the villagers put into restoring it."

He was across the room in quick strides. He caught her hand between both of his. "You misunderstand. It isn't my home I'm worried about, my lady. It's you."

The fact that he would be worried over her had her blushing furiously. She was so startled by his concern, she could only stare. "I'll be fine."

"Aye. You will. Very fine indeed." He studied the high color, loving the way her lashes fluttered as she avoided his eyes.

For a moment she thought he might kiss her lips once more. Her heart actually fluttered at the thought. Instead, he lifted her hands to his lips and kissed first one, then the other, lingering over them as though she were a great lady.

A series of tremors sliced down her spine, leaving her feeling oddly disoriented.

"My lord…"

"My lady." He lifted his head and captured her chin in his hand, brushing a butterfly kiss over her lips.

She felt the quick rush of heat, and the way a pulse fluttered in her throat. What amazing powers he had, that he could so affect her with the simple press of his mouth on hers.

When he lifted his head, he stared deeply into her eyes before releasing her and striding swiftly out the door.

Minutes later she heard the sound of his horse's hoof beats in the courtyard. And then silence closed in around her.

She pressed a hand to her heart, wondering at the way it thundered. She could still taste him on her lips.

How was it that such a simple thing as two mouths touching could create such a storm inside her?

She dragged in several deep breaths, wondering at the sudden feeling of light-headedness. She felt as she often did when one of her spells went wrong.

Squaring her shoulders, she decided that what she needed was to be busy. She would use this time alone to have a long visit with those who lay in the garden under their fresh mounds of earth. Perhaps it would be best if she began chronicling their requests, so as not to forget any. After all, this was so new to her, she was certain there would be plenty of mistakes made along the way. Especially in light of her history of missteps.

Now if only she could keep her mind on her work, and away from a certain dark, dangerous warrior.

"I was the cook at Ross Abbey for two score years, my lady."

Though the woman standing in the garden atop her grave appeared no more than ten and eight, Gwenellen wasn't surprised. After visiting with the newly-buried for several hours, she was gradually adjusting to the fact that most of them had assumed the image of a time in their lives when they'd been young and vital.

"What is it you'd like me to attend to?"

The woman pursed her lips. *"There is a crofter in the village who owes me a debt of two lambs from his flock. My son and his wife could use those lambs, but since they know nothing of the debt, I fear it will go unpaid."*

"Would you prefer that I speak with your son, or the crofter?"

"The crofter." The woman gave a cackling laugh that rang in the still air. *"And I'd like to see his eyes when he hears that ye've talked with me."*

Gwenellen joined the woman's laughter. "Give me his name, and I'll see that it's done."

The woman patted her hand. *"Ye're a fine lass.*

It's glad I am that the young laird has ye on his side, my lady.''

"You think well of the lord?"

"Oh, aye. He was a good lad, and has grown into a fine man. Not that I'm surprised. His father and mother were kind and generous with all who met them.''

Gwenellen looked up at a clatter in the courtyard and watched as several wagons and carts came to a halt.

She turned to bid goodbye to the cook and found her image already fading from sight.

By the time she walked to the courtyard, Andrew was instructing a score of men and women, lads and lasses in their duties.

When he spotted her he stepped forward and placed a hand beneath her elbow, leading her toward the others.

"The lady Gwenellen of the clan Drummond will be staying at Ross Abbey. Her comfort is to be your primary concern."

She felt her cheeks flame at the looks that ranged from speculative to disapproving.

Andrew seemed to take no notice. "My lady, this is Mistress MacLean. She is wed to my most trusted warrior, Drymen MacLean, and is cousin to Duncan. She helped cook at the tavern, and has agreed to serve as housekeeper."

The woman was nearly as tall as Andrew, with jet-black hair pulled into a severe knot at her nape. Her gown was clean and crisp, her hands workworn. The look she gave Gwenellen was one of disapproval.

She gave a stiff nod of her head. "My lady."

Gwenellen managed a smile. "Mistress Mac-Lean."

The new housekeeper pinched the arm of a shy, dark-haired lass and gave her a shove forward. "This is Olnore, who will be your maidservant."

"Olnore." Taking pity on the sweet child, Gwenellen deliberately kept her tone gentle. "I look forward to your help."

The girl's gaze darted to the housekeeper, who had everyone quaking in fear, then back to this exotic woman who had everyone in the village abuzz with speculation. Where had she come from? And why was the lord so concerned for her comfort?

Andrew beckoned to a giant, who stepped away from the others. "This is Lloyd, who will see to the stables and horses."

"Lloyd." Gwenellen had to tip back her head to see the man's ruddy face, framed by a thatch of russet hair.

"And his son, Paine, who will help around the castle."

"Paine." Gwenellen could see the resemblance between father and son. Both stood head and shoulders above the others in the courtyard. Both had pale blue eyes and cheeks as red as their hair.

Andrew turned to her. "There will be others. Mistress MacLean has agreed to find enough servants to see to all the needs of the household."

"That's very kind of you, Mistress."

The woman fixed Gwenellen with a stare. "The old laird was good to us. We'll do no less for his son, the new laird." She waved an arm at those standing around. "Inside with you now. The day is fleeting."

That was all it took to send the servants scrambling.

When they were alone in the courtyard, Andrew turned to Gwenellen. "Did you have another visit with my father while I was gone?"

She shook her head. "Nay. But there were others." She told him about the cook and the debt owed to her family.

The mention of her had Andrew smiling. "After my mother died, Cook used to bake my favorite biscuits. She'd drizzle them with honey, or top them with clotted cream and berries. Whenever I walked into the refectory, there would be a treat awaiting me. I thought of her as my special friend here at Ross Abbey. Looking back, I can see how much her kindness meant to a lonely lad who'd lost his mother to sudden death."

"Now I'm doubly glad to see to her request." Gwenellen studied the man beside her. "How old were you when your mother died?"

"Nine. She took a fever, and within days was gone from us." He thought a minute before adding, "I don't know who missed her more. My father was inconsolable. As for me, within the year I was sent off to apprentice as a warrior, and I managed to bury my grief in fighting."

That had Gwenellen shaking her head in wonder. "Is this how all in your world deal with grief?"

He chuckled. "I doubt the women would take to the life of a warrior. But there is something to be said for hard, demanding challenges to take the mind off heartache." He glanced at her. "How do you deal with it in your world?"

"I wouldn't know. I've never suffered grief, or as you refer to it, heartache."

"Never?"

She felt an odd little tingling at the way he was watching her. "I felt sadness when my sisters left me."

"Why did they leave?"

"To live with the Highland lords who claimed their hearts."

He seemed suddenly alert. "They are wed to mortals?"

"Aye." She wrinkled her nose. "They speak about their lives now the way they once spoke about life in our kingdom. As though it were some grand adventure."

"Perhaps it is. It sounds as though they are truly in love with their husbands."

"Love." She turned away. "I know nothing of such things. I know only that life is different in my kingdom since they left."

"Different? In what way?"

"The days seem longer. My pleasures…less intense, now that I can no longer share them."

"Ah." He nodded in understanding. "You miss them."

"Perhaps." She didn't like talking about such things. It always caused an unpleasant sting around her heart. "I believe I'll see if Mistress MacLean could use my help."

As she flounced into the castle, he followed more slowly. It would seem that even witches could feel loneliness and sorrow. And best of all, love.

Even toward mortals.

He had no idea why that idea should please him so. But please him it did. Not that he had any intention of losing his heart again. A wise man learned from his mistakes. Still, it was pleasant to think that witches and mortals could love.

He returned to his labors with a lighter heart.

Chapter Eight

"You must hurry and dress for dinner, my lady." Breathless, Olnore hurried into Gwenellen's chambers.

Gwenellen turned from the balcony, where she'd been watching the flight of a falcon. How grand it would be to stretch out her arms and fly. She sighed, missing her winged horse, and the many flights she took in the company of Jeremy. But at least she could be content in the knowledge that her family wouldn't be worried about her.

"Why must I dress for dinner, Olnore? What's wrong with what I'm wearing?"

The little servant wrinkled her nose. "Mistress MacLean said that when the old laird was alive, dinner in the great hall was always a grand occasion. Now that Lord Andrew is laird, it is important that custom be followed."

Gwenellen looked down at the wrinkled skirt of her gown. "This is all I have, Olnore."

"Nay, my lady." The servant pointed to the array of garments hanging on hooks along the wall. "Lord Andrew said you are to make use of all of these. Whatever is in these chambers now belongs to you."

Gwenellen cast a dubious glance at the gowns in rich hues of crimson and sapphire and emerald. "I don't feel right wearing the clothes of a woman being held hostage. What if she should return and take offense?"

Olnore lifted a gown of soft burnished gold from a hook and held it up for her inspection. "I would much prefer the wrath of Lady Sabrina later, to that of Mistress MacLean this night."

That had Gwenellen laughing. She found the little servant's sense of humor delightful. Still smiling, she removed her gown and allowed herself to be dressed. A short time later she arrived at the great hall, where Andrew stood alone in front of a blazing fire.

Seeing her, it seemed to take him a moment to pull himself back from the bleak thoughts that darkened his gaze. "Will you have some ale, my lady?"

"Aye, thank you."

He filled a tumbler from a decanter. When he handed it to her their fingers brushed and he absorbed the warmth that always seemed to accompany her touch. Though he sensed that it was due to her witchcraft, it didn't make it any easier to ignore.

She glanced around. "I thought there would be guests for dinner."

He frowned. "You mean, because of Mistress MacLean's insistence upon the proper order of things?"

"Aye."

He nodded. "She's a bit pompous. But she's right, I suppose. As laird, I must abide by rules that often annoyed me when I was simply the laird's heir. But I'm not yet ready to entertain guests."

She couldn't fault him for that. It was too soon since the death of all the people he'd known and loved. She struggled for ways to keep his mind off his sorrow. "Did you find it difficult being the son of a laird?"

"At times. In the company of rough and tumble friends from the village, I demanded to be treated like one of them. But I knew that, while they returned to humble cottages, my home was a castle where there was always enough to eat. Where there were servants to do my bidding. As the only child, I never had to fight for my father's attention. I was fortunate that, growing up, we rarely had a disagreement. At least not until…" He frowned and turned away.

Gwenellen wondered at the sudden look in his eyes, in that moment before he'd turned from her. When he turned back, he was composed.

"Forgive me, my lady. Why don't you sit here by the fire?"

She settled herself on the chaise and was dismayed when he sat beside her. The mere brush of his thigh against hers, and the touch of his shoulder to hers, had warmth spreading through her veins.

"The fire is very warm, isn't it?" She sipped her ale and wished with all her might that someone would join them. Someone who might distract her from her disquieting thoughts.

"Is it? I hadn't noticed." But he'd noticed the way her breasts strained the bodice of her gown. And the way the color complemented her eyes, turning them to liquid gold.

Not that she tried to be noticed. On the contrary, he had the impression that she would much prefer to be invisible. It was as though she were uncomfortable in his company, though he hadn't yet figured out why. He'd never before had quite that effect on a woman. But then, she wasn't like other women. At least none he'd ever known.

They both looked up when the housekeeper entered, followed by a column of servants.

Mistress MacLean stood like a warrior about to do battle. "Dinner is served, my laird."

With a sigh Andrew stood and offered his arm. Gwenellen placed her hand on his sleeve and together they crossed the room to the enormous table which seemed even bigger when set for two.

Andrew held her chair, then settled himself beside her.

The servants circled the table, offering food from gleaming silver trays.

Gwenellen accepted a serving of fish and one of fowl. Andrew did the same, then waved the servants away. At a signal from the housekeeper they disappeared, leaving the lord and his lady alone.

"What do you eat in your kingdom, my lady?"

"Much the same as you eat here. Fish from the Enchanted Loch. Fowl. Deer. Fresh vegetables from our garden. And our wonderful roseberries."

"I'm not familiar with roseberries."

"I'm told they grow only in our kingdom." She looked down. "I confess I have a weakness for them. As does Jeremy."

"Is that so?" He leaned back, his feast forgotten. There was something about the sound of her voice. It was soft as a sigh, with a slightly breathless quality that did strange things to him. He wanted to keep her talking, so he could indulge himself. "Do you have any other weaknesses I ought to know about?"

"I have a sweet tooth. I love anything sweet. Scones, tarts and Bessie's wonderful currant cake, topped with clotted cream and berries."

"Could you teach our cook to bake them?"

She shook her head, sending honey curls dancing. "Bessie says I'm hopeless in the kitchen. Mum says the same about my sewing and weaving. I remember the time I was given the task of mending a gown I'd torn while climbing trees."

"Climbing trees? I thought all lasses did was play in the meadow and make daisy chains."

She wrinkled her nose. "How dull. I much prefer playing high in the trees with the fairies, or flying on Starlight's back among the clouds."

He couldn't help grinning. "Of course. How could I forget? So," he prompted, "you were given the task of mending your gown."

"Aye. But I hated sewing, and the day was so pretty, and I was eager to find Jeremy. So I cast a spell, ordering the gown mended, then went off on a grand adventure with my friend."

"The troll." He didn't know why the thought of this imp spending her days with a troll should amuse him so, but the mere thought had his grin widening. "And just what was your grand adventure?"

"We filled an entire bucket with roseberries, then sat in the heather and ate all of them without getting sick. Afterward we played hide-and-seek among the clouds on Starlight and Moonlight, and I won. Best of all, I went for a swim in the loch, while Jeremy watched from shore." She laughed at the memory. "Trolls hate water."

"I see." He was laughing, too. He couldn't help it. She was just so delightfully fresh.

She sobered. "Of course we hurried home in time for supper. We were rarely late for a meal. But when we got there, Bessie was nowhere to be found. The fire had burned out—the kettle cold. When Mum and

Gram returned from tending Allegra's garden, they took one look and knew I'd shirked my duty. Mum said, 'You lazy child. Rather than bother to sew, you cast one of your spells, didn't you?' I knew there and then I was in trouble. So did Jeremy.''

"How did your mother know about the spell?"

Avoiding his eyes, Gwenellen traced a finger along the curl of lace on the fine cloth beside her plate. "I'd failed to look up. If I had, I'd have seen poor old Bessie floating among the clouds, wrapped in my torn gown."

"In the clouds? What caused her to float?"

She shrugged. "A little misstep on my part."

"A misstep?" He bit back the laughter that had begun to rumble deep in his chest.

"I was certain I'd asked for a gown made anew, and instead was given a maid gone askew." She brought her hands to her lap. "Or something to that effect."

He covered his mouth and stifled a chuckle. "How long was poor Bessie up in the air?"

"Most of the day. Poor thing. She…suffers from dizziness when she even steps on a stool."

There was no holding back the laughter now. It roared up from deep inside and bellowed forth. Between peals of laughter he managed to ask, "How did you get her down?"

"Mum cast a spell. By the time the poor old dear

was back on the ground, her head was spinning so, she had to be helped to her bed.''

The image had him laughing all the harder. "I'll bet she wasn't too happy with you. How did you make it up to her?"

"I promised to do all her chores for a week. But after only a day, she said she'd never recover her strength if she had to continue to eat the swill I called cooking.''

"Oh, my lady. You're such a delight.'' He closed a hand over hers. "Tell me. Are there many more stories like this one?"

"Scores of them, I fear.'' Though she'd initially been embarrassed to admit her foolishness, she now found herself laughing along with him.

He squeezed her hand just as Mistress MacLean and the servants returned to offer second helpings.

Leaning close he muttered, "I want to hear every one of them.''

As he accepted bread warm from the oven, he realized his heart felt lighter than it had in months. He glanced at the woman beside him and knew it was because of her. Just listening to that soft, breathy voice that seemed to wrap itself around his heart and whisper over his senses, had him feeling wonderfully relaxed.

"Tell me more about your home, my lord. Why is it called an abbey?''

"One of my ancestors lost her lover on the field

of battle, and vowed to never love again. She received permission from her father to set aside a portion of the estate for a chapel and abbey, to study in the company of holy women. When the countryside was overrun by barbarians, the castle was destroyed and all inside were murdered. But when the barbarians attempted to storm the abbey, they were repelled by some unseen force.''

Fascinated, Gwenellen sipped her ale. "An unseen force? Were these holy women gifted with…certain powers?''

Andrew arched a brow. "There have been rumors of that through the ages. But of course, no one knows for certain." He broke open a biscuit, attempting to push aside the little doubt that had suddenly crept in to tease him. It had been easy to ignore such things when he'd been convinced that there were no such things as witches. Now, he realized many of the things he'd held as myth might, in fact, be truth. "My ancestors never rebuilt the ancient abbey, choosing instead to add on a fortress which is the current castle."

"If that be true, then we are on holy ground, my lord." Gwenellen spoke softly, to keep from being overheard by the servants.

He shook his head. "I know nothing of that. But it is my home, and I have no intention of seeing it overrun by invaders again." He waved aside a servant who approached with more food. "Would you care for anything else, my lady?"

"Nay." She was too excited to think about food. No wonder her gift was so strong, so sure, here in this place. This man's ancestor had been one of the ancient ones blessed with very special gifts. Of that she was certain.

"You're suddenly quiet, my lady."

Andrew's voice brought her out of her thoughts. "I was enjoying this fine food and the warmth of this place."

He glanced around, trying to see his home through her eyes. "It is warm and comforting. Always, when I returned from the field of battle, I felt a sense of peace at arriving home. But I'm not certain if it was the building itself, or the people who lived here."

"You were close to your father?"

"Aye. I suppose losing my mother at such a tender age, we drew strength from one another, because of our shared grief."

"He waited a long time to take another wife."

She saw Andrew's smile fade and regretted her words. But it was too late. The wonderful smile was gone, and that dark, brooding frown was back as he picked up his tankard, draining it in one long swallow.

At once a servant approached and refilled it.

The housekeeper led a wench to the table and removed a linen covering from the tray she held. "Cook has made custard tarts, my lord."

"None for me, thank you." His tone was curt as he turned to Gwenellen. "Would you try the sweets, my lady?"

She shook her head, still feeling remorse at having spoiled his mood.

"Thank you, Mistress MacLean." Abruptly he stood and offered his arm to the young woman beside him. "You'll convey my thanks to Cook?"

"Aye, my lord." The housekeeper signaled for the servants to stand aside until Andrew and Gwenellen took their leave of the great hall.

At the foot of the stairs Andrew bowed over Gwenellen's hand. "I go now to my father's old chambers to see to the ledgers. If you require anything, you need only ask a servant."

"Thank you." She watched him walk away, then, feeling oddly bereft, she turned in the opposite direction.

For a little while he'd actually appeared to be enjoying himself. She would have sworn he liked hearing about her home, her childhood in the Mystical Kingdom. But she'd spoiled everything by mentioning his father's wife.

Though Andrew's happiness, or lack of it, should mean nothing to her, she found herself brooding over it.

He ought to smile more often. When he did, he

was so handsome and charming, he nearly stole her breath.

She stopped in midstride and touched a hand to her heart. Whatever was she thinking? He was a mortal. A Highland warrior, who admitted to spending a lifetime in battle. She was not like her sisters, content to sit by the fire and wait for their men to return from war. She had no intention of staying in this place another day longer than was required of her.

Still, she couldn't deny the little thrill she felt whenever he touched her. Why was that? Was this a power that all mortals possessed? Or was Andrew Ross different?

Annoyed with the way her thoughts kept circling back to him, she lifted her skirts, intent upon exploring the castle, and filling her mind with something other than the lord of Ross Abbey.

Chapter Nine

Gwenellen's footsteps were muted as she walked along the garden path. Moonlight filtered through the branches of the trees, casting the ground before her in a kaleidoscope of light and shadow. Already the scent of charred wood and death was beginning to fade, replaced by the fragrance of roses just coming into bloom. Soon, she thought, the abbey would be restored to its former beauty. But the horror of what had happened here would not soon be forgotten, especially by the new laird.

As she passed the fresh graves, she waited for the voices, but this night they were strangely silent.

Moving along the curving strip of grass, she looked up. By the flicker of candlelight from the second-story balcony, she could see Andrew as he sat at his father's desk, bent over the ledgers. She stood very still, studying his profile. He wasn't so much handsome as rugged. With that wide brow and stern demeanor, and that lock of dark hair that seemed always in need of being brushed aside, there was a look of danger to him. But when he smiled, it was as though a torch had been held to a score of candles inside him, lighting not only his eyes, but also his soul.

He was, she knew, a good man, held in high esteem by his people. And if he thought too often about vengeance, it was understandable. Perhaps his father's spirit would persist, and the cycle of violence would be ended.

A sudden chill breeze stirred the leaves and sent her scurrying back to the abbey in search of her shawl. Once inside she moved along the hallway, too restless to retire to her chambers.

Outside a massive door she paused, and read the ancient words carved into the wood.

"Let all who enter know the wisdom of truth." Her voice was hushed as she deciphered their meaning aloud before stepping inside.

Logs lay on the grate, and many more beside it. No fire burned on the hearth, yet the room bore no chill. A fur-covered chaise was pulled close to the fireplace, inviting a cozy spot in which to rest. Instead of crossed swords hanging above the mantel, it seemed to be some sort of ancient wood carved into the shape of a circle. The sight of shelves soaring several stories to the wooden-beamed rafters high above had her sucking in a breath. The shelves were filled with books. So many books. She'd never known there could be this many in one place. Such an amazing store of knowledge, and all of it available to those who lived within these walls.

She touched a hand to the leather bindings. They were coated with dust, attesting to the fact that they hadn't been used in a very long time.

Though the rest of the abbey had been torched, this room showed no effect from the fire. Not a single book seemed to be scorched. Was that why the servants hadn't cleaned this room, or even bothered to lay a fire on the hearth?

Or could there be another reason? Were they afraid to enter? Could this be the room where the holy women met to share their knowledge?

A study of the titles of the books confirmed her suspicions. Written in the ancient tongues, they translated to *The Art Of Ancient Healing. Calling Down The Spirits. Chants That Heal. Spells That Guard Against The Evil Ones.*

As Gwenellen prowled the room, she caught sight of a spill of moonlight through a high, narrow window. It slanted on a leather-bound book just under the rafters. Unlike the others, dark with age and thick with dust, this one shimmered, pale and iridescent, like a beacon that called to her.

A shiver passed through her, and she knew, in that instant, that she had to have this book. It was, she sensed, the font of ancient secrets. It would tell her all the things she needed to know to hone her gifts to perfection.

But how was she to get it?

As an idea came to her she glanced around, making certain that there were no servants in the hallway. Seeing no one, she extended her arms, closed her eyes, and began to chant the ancient words.

When she'd finished, she opened her eyes. "I command you, take me high. To yonder shelf I wish to fly."

The minute the words were out of her mouth she lifted ever-so-lightly off the floor and began soaring toward the high wooden beams.

Pleased with herself, she relaxed, ready to enjoy the ride. When she was level with the highest shelf she reached out for the book that shimmered and pulsed with an inner glow.

The moment her hands closed around it, she was aware that something had gone terribly wrong. The power deserted her, and she started to drop like a stone. Desperate, she grabbed onto the shelf and was able to hang on, barely, by her fingertips.

The book crashed to the floor far below and was forgotten as she strained to keep from tumbling after it. Sweat beaded her brow as she struggled to tighten her grasp on the edge of the shelf. But with each breath that wheezed from between her parted lips, she could feel herself slipping.

She chanced a look down. At once the room spun

and she felt the dizziness take hold. She closed her eyes and swallowed back the nausea that threatened. With each breath, her slick fingers slid closer to the edge of the shelf, threatening to dash her to the cold stone floor.

Even if she managed to survive a fall from this distance, she had no doubt that she would suffer broken bones, as well as a great deal of pain.

Andrew shoved away from his father's desk and pressed a hand to the back of his neck. He resented the amount of time needed to balance the abbey's ledgers. It was a task his father had accepted with good nature, and one Andrew found tedious and annoying. Column after column of numbers that had to be tallied. Flocks of sheep and herds of cattle to be divided. Crops to be harvested and distributed among the clan.

He wanted to be a good and honest laird to his people. But the task seemed overwhelming. He needed to see that every widow and orphan was given a place in his household, so that they wouldn't have to worry about their next meal, or the coming winter. He would have to train those men who remained, those too young and those far too old, in the art of defending their land and people, before their enemies returned.

That part, at least, appealed to him. He was more

comfortable with a sword in his hand than a quill and parchment.

Seeing movement in the garden he strode to the balcony and watched as Gwenellen moved slowly along the path. From this distance she appeared other-worldly, with moonlight turning her hair to spun gold, and a sprinkling of stardust at her feet. She paused and he thought she was looking up at him. Could almost feel the warmth of her touch as it slid ever-so-softly over him.

Had he imagined that touch? If so, why did the warmth linger on his flesh?

Stepping back, he watched until she disappeared beneath the balcony and stepped into the abbey.

The ledgers were forgotten. What he wanted, what he craved more than life itself at this moment, was to hear her voice. To see her face. To touch her.

Aye. He needed to touch her. Now. This very moment.

He strode from the room and descended the great stairs. When he reached the main level he never paused, but was drawn along the hallway until he stopped in front of the open doorway leading to the ancient library.

He stepped inside, his eyes adjusting to the gloom. What he saw had his heart stopping. Gwenellen was hanging by her fingertips from the very top shelf, just beneath the rafters.

He was across the room in quick strides. His voice,

when he finally found it, was gruff, but he was determined to hide his fear from her, lest it make things worse. "Fancy finding you here, my lady."

Gwenellen looked down, eyes wild, voice little more than a breathy whisper. "Thank heaven you're here. Can you help me? I fear I can't hold on any longer."

He glanced around, hoping for a ladder. Seeing none, he sighed in frustration. "How did you get up there?"

"I tried one of my spells. It seems to have…gone awry."

"I see. Why not try another and get yourself down from there?"

"I'm afraid I might find myself in even graver peril than I am now."

"For once you seem to have shown a bit of wisdom." In a glance he gauged the distance, the danger, then planted his feet. "Let go, my lady, and I'll catch you."

"I can't."

"You must."

She shook her head, and even that simple movement brought her to the very edge of the shelf. She scrambled for a better grasp, but could feel herself slipping. "From this distance I'm likely to kill us both."

"I'll just have to take that chance. Let go, my lady." His tone hardened. "Now."

Gwenellen had no choice. At that very moment she felt herself slipping free and falling, falling. She waited for the crash, the pain. Instead, just before she hit the floor, she was caught in arms of steel and engulfed in warmth.

Andrew held her close and pressed his lips to her temple, willing his heartbeat to steady. He'd thought, in that one terrible moment before impact, that he'd misjudged, and would drop her. He'd seen, in his mind's eye, the look of her, dashed upon the stone floor and shattered like a helpless bird. It had wrenched his heart as nothing else could have.

He masked his fear with anger. "Little fool. What were you thinking?"

Feeling the sting of his hot breath on her cheek, Gwenellen was awash in so many emotions. Shame. Fear. And a great welling of relief that she'd been saved from her own folly.

When at last she found her voice, she managed to whisper, "There was a book. On the highest shelf."

"A book?" Still holding her in his arms, he waved a hand. "There are hundreds of them. Why did you have to choose one that posed such risk?"

"It was different. All light and shimmering. It…called to me."

"It called to you?" He looked down at this woman in his arms, wondering if his heart would ever stop thundering. It was a miracle it didn't burst clean through his chest. "It would appear, my lady, that you are in need of a keeper, for you seem determined to harm yourself.''

Stung, she pushed free of his arms. Though her legs trembled she stood her ground. ''And I suppose you see yourself as so much wiser.''

''Wise enough not to attempt to fly. If you'd been meant for such things, you'd have been given wings.'' Without thinking he dragged her close. In his eyes was a dark, almost frightening look. ''Sweet heaven, you could have been killed.''

''Aye. And then you'd have been rid of me, my lord.''

''Don't say such things. Don't even think…''

The very air between them seemed to shimmer and stir, as though charged by some unseen force.

With a savage oath he covered her mouth with his.

The kiss caught them both by surprise. All fire and flash and need, it pulsed between them with the shattering force of a summer storm. A strike by lightning would have been less shocking. Their heartbeats thundered in their chests, causing them to struggle for breath.

Andrew drank her in deeply before lifting his head and drawing back, stunned by the depth of feeling that had welled up, unbidden, at the first touch of her. His eyes narrowed on hers, and he could read the fear and confusion. And something more. The awakening of a deep, slumbering desire. It touched him deeply.

He framed her face with his hands. His voice lowered to a moan. ''I was so afraid for you.''

There was such passion in his voice. The depth of his feelings startled her.

Before she could reply he plunged his hands into the tangles of her hair, drawing it back as he covered her mouth in a kiss so searing, so hungry, he nearly devoured her.

He felt her stiffen for just a moment. Then her body seemed to go pliant. Her mouth softened, opening to him. Her hands reached out blindly, clutching his waist, as she returned his kisses with a hunger, a passion that matched his.

''You were afraid, too, my lord?''

''Aye.'' He ran hot, nibbling kisses over her upturned face. Her eyes, her cheeks, the tip of her nose.

Gwenellen wondered at the way her heartbeat began racing, as though she'd just been running across a meadow at breakneck speed. Her mind filled with images so erotic she could feel her cheeks burning. There were so many strange needs tumbling about inside her.

His voice was a growl of frustration as he trailed his lips down the smooth column of her throat. ''You must promise never to frighten me like that again.''

''I…'' She couldn't get the words out. Her throat was so constricted, she feared she might embarrass herself by bursting into tears.

"Promise me, my lady. For I couldn't bear to see you harmed."

"I'll do my best." She stood very still, loving the feel of his arms around her. Of that warm, clever mouth brushing kisses over her face. And those hands. So big and strong, moving along her back, setting fires wherever they touched.

She had the most overpowering need to be loved by this man. To be cherished. For the first time in her life it didn't matter that she couldn't control her powers. What mattered was that Andrew had worried over her. Not out of annoyance, but out of... something deeper.

Oh, what was the matter with her? Hadn't she vowed never to lose her heart to a mortal as her sisters had done? And yet here she was, not only permitting this mortal to kiss her, to hold her, but wanting him to. And wanting more. Wanting all those things that Allegra and Kylia had found with their mortals.

She knew she ought to demand that he stop, but instead she held on tightly as he took her on a wild ride of emotions that left her even more confused and dizzy than when she'd been hanging by her fingertips in midair.

Andrew reminded himself that the woman in his arms was an innocent. He had no right to these liberties. But how could he stop, when she tasted like heaven? When the touch of her aroused him as no woman's touch ever had?

He'd thought, for one brief moment, that she was lost to him. And then she'd landed like an angel in his arms, and the joy he'd felt was beyond belief. It was more than joy. It was pure jubilation. His heart was close to bursting with it.

He took the kiss deeper, loving the feel of her lips on his. There was a taste about her, a sweetness, that had him thinking about lush, exotic lands and forbidden fruit. He savored the feel of her body against his. All soft curves that melted into him as though made for him alone.

"Andrew." She lifted a finger to his cheek.

In reply his hands tangled in her hair, drawing her head back as he ran open-mouth kisses down her throat. He ached to touch her everywhere. To feel her body move under his. He felt himself being drawn down into the dark, primitive need to take her, here, now, like a savage.

He was trembling when he lifted his head and held her a little away.

"Forgive me, my lady."

Her breathing was too ragged to form a reply. She merely stared at him as he released her and took a step back.

"It's late. I'll see you to your chambers."

"There's no need." She drew herself up and stepped around him, eager to escape those dark, knowing eyes. Was it possible that he could see into her heart? Could he read her most intimate thoughts? Did he know how much she wanted him to do more than kiss her, touch her?

"I believe I can manage the stairs without doing harm." She flung the words without a backward glance, and hurried away.

When she was gone, he caught a glimpse of the book lying on the floor at his feet. He bent to retrieve it. Not bright and shimmering, as she'd described it, but a dark, dusty collection of parchment so fragile it appeared to crumble as he set it on a low shelf. Then his gaze moved upward to the shelf high above. The sight of it had him shuddering, for it was high enough that the fall could have broken her neck.

"Fool," he muttered as he walked away.

But he wasn't certain just who was the bigger fool. She'd merely risked her life. If he kept this up, he'd be risking something far greater. And his heart was something he'd vowed never again to risk.

Gwenellen's heart was still racing when she reached her chambers. Once inside she paused and took several deep breaths before facing the servant who hurried over to take her shawl.

She wanted desperately to be alone. To sort out all these strange new emotions swirling around in her mind, making her feel as she'd felt that first time, so many years ago, when she'd climbed on Starlight's back and had soared among the clouds. Aye, that was it exactly. She was soaring. Not from a simple ride on a winged horse, but from something so much more grand. A kiss. A kiss that had left her wildly unsettled and hungry for more.

"You seem out of breath, my lady." Olnore led the way to the sleeping chambers, where the bed linens had already been turned down.

"I took a walk in the gardens." Gwenellen stifled a giggle. If she were to walk there now, her feet would surely never touch the ground.

How could one man's mouth be so firm, and yet so tempting? What was it about his arms that could make her feel so safe, and at the same time, so deliciously wicked?

"I took a walk there myself, not half an hour ago." Olnore seemed to take a very long time folding the shawl and setting it aside.

"I didn't see you, Olnore. Were you alone?"

"Nay, my lady. I was...with Paine."

"Lloyd's son?"

"Aye, my lady."

Gwenellen saw the slight flush that colored the servant's cheeks and felt a sudden kinship with this young woman. Did the two hold hands as they walked? Had they kissed in the shadows?

"Oh, my lady, you've soiled your gown."

"My gown?" Gwenellen's thoughts scattered. She glanced down with a look of guilt. The bodice of her gown bore the dust of the bookshelves, as did her hands. "After my walk I found a room filled with books. They've been neglected, and seemed quite dusty."

"That would be the library of the old abbey, my lady." Olnore reached for the buttons of Gwenellen's gown. "The servants are unwilling to work in there." She lowered her voice. "'Tis said there are strange things in the old section of the abbey."

"What sort of things?" As if she cared. Right now the only thing she could think about, care about, was Andrew, and that warm, clever mouth.

The little servant shrugged. "There were whispers in the village from those who worked here. Of shadowy figures of robed women long dead, reading from their books and chanting in the night." She removed Gwenellen's gown and reached for the nightdress, slipping it over her head. "One of the servants swore she saw the old laird's first wife standing in the doorway."

Gwenellen wondered what the serving wench would say if she knew that her mistress not only saw the dead, but could speak with them. Tonight, however, it wasn't the dead that held Gwenellen's interest, but the living. And soon, very soon, she would be alone with her thoughts, able to relive in glorious detail that surprising scene in the abbey.

She yawned, hoping the little servant would soon take her leave. Lowering her hands to the basin of water, she washed, then reached for a clean linen towel. "Will you return to the garden now, Olnore, or will you sleep?"

"I'll go to my bed now, my lady. But on the morrow, when my chores are done, I'll most likely walk in the garden again." Her voice softened. "If Paine should invite me."

"I see." Gwenellen settled into her bed and the servant tucked the linens around her.

Minutes later the candle was snuffed and the door closed softly.

In the darkness Gwenellen lay, allowing the scene in the library to play through her mind.

"Oh, Gram." Her voice was little more than a sigh. "I know I scoffed at my sisters when they lost their hearts to Highland warriors. But Andrew Ross is different. Not only because he's kind and good and noble. But when he touches me, I feel safe. Protected. You should have seen him, Gram, when he caught me just as I was about to be dashed against the stone floor. He was…magnificent. I know he would never permit any harm to befall me."

She shivered at the thought of those strong arms catching her, enfolding her.

And drifted into sleep, still tasting him on her lips.

Chapter Ten

"My lord." Gwenellen paused to catch her breath.

She'd spent a restless night, and then had slept until the sun was high in the sky. While breaking her fast on her balcony she'd caught sight of Andrew in the high meadow, surrounded by a cluster of men and boys.

She wasn't so much eager to be near him, she told herself, as merely curious. That would explain why she'd run the entire distance. And it wasn't the nearness of him that had her heart thundering; it was the exertion of that run.

Despite the serious nature of this training, Andrew found himself distracted by the sight of yellow curls dancing around a pixie face. A face that never failed to stir his heart.

He lowered his sword and walked toward her.

"You shouldn't be here. I'm teaching the villagers how to be warriors."

She looked around and realized that most of the men from the village, both young and old, were here, and all of them carrying an assortment of weapons. Some held rusted swords and dull knives. Others had hoes, scythes, sickles and any number of farm implements.

She lowered her voice so the others wouldn't hear. "You would ignore your father's wishes?"

"You've told me what's in his heart. Unfortunately, since I can't know what is in Fergus Logan's heart, I think it best to prepare the villagers for an attack. Since I've heard no word from my warriors in Edinburgh, I have no choice but to arm the villagers, and hope to teach them in mere days what it's taken me a lifetime to learn. If they can't be warriors, at least they can defend themselves against an assault." He gave her a measured look. "You need not be afraid. I'll see you're kept safe, my lady."

She lifted her head. "I'm not afraid, my lord. I merely wonder why you seem so…eager for battle."

"Is that what you think? That I enjoy killing?" His easy smile faded.

"I mean no disapproval." She hated the fact that his smile was gone. And that she was the one who'd erased it. "But once you have an army, it would be tempting to confront your enemy with a display of strength.''

''Tempting, perhaps. But I'm no fool. I may be laird, but I'm also a warrior, trained for any eventuality. Only a fool would wait complacently for his enemy to return, without making plans for the safety of his people.''

That made sense.

She brightened. ''Perhaps I could help.''

''You think to teach the lads how to wield a sword?'' He held the weapon alongside her, measuring her against it. ''My sword is bigger than you.'' At her little pout he added, ''And then there are all those rusted knife blades. Perhaps you could conjure a spell that would sharpen them?''

''I believe you're having fun with me, my lord.''

He leaned close. ''How can I not?'' He saw the way her cheeks colored and allowed himself to touch a finger there before taking a step back. ''Go and join the women. If you really wish to be helpful, perhaps you could persuade Mistress MacLean to serve our supper in someplace other than that drafty great hall.''

''Would you prefer the library in the old section of the abbey?''

That had him thinking about the kiss they'd shared. He kept his features deliberately bland. But there was a hint of danger in his eyes before he turned away. ''Since the servants are afraid to go in there, I doubt even your considerable charm could persuade Mistress MacLean of that.''

''Perhaps I'll try a spell to persuade your house-keeper, my lord.''

He paused. Turned. ''I'd say it's your duty as a witch. But only as a last resort. Remember the consequences.''

As she danced away, she could feel him watching her. The thought had her laughing in delight.

Oh, it was so grand to feel this way. And she thought she might not be alone in her feelings. He had to care for her, at least a little. Hadn't he kissed her?

But had he spent the entire night thinking about the kisses they'd shared? Had he tossed and turned and remembered every touch, every word, as she had?

When she arrived back at the abbey she went in search of the housekeeper, hoping to persuade her that the laird would be greatly pleased to sup in the library. And hoping she wouldn't have to resort to a spell, since there was no telling where that might land them both.

''Mistress MacLean.'' Gwenellen found the housekeeper overseeing a staff of young women from the village who were cleaning and polishing the scarred wooden tables in the great hall. ''In the event of an attack by enemies, what are the women and children expected to do?''

The older woman shrugged. ''Without the protection of the laird's warriors, there's not much we can do, except hope our men are able to defend us.''

''But surely there are things we can do to help ourselves.'' Gwenellen began to pace. ''Does everyone take shelter in the abbey?''

''Aye, my lady.''

''Is there room for the entire village?''

''There is. It will be crowded, but tolerable.''

At the housekeeper's words, Gwenellen came to a decision. ''Then we must see to their comfort. There are many unused rooms in the abbey that can be put to good use as sleeping chambers. Perhaps the women of the village should begin weaving cloth for pallets and blankets.'' She could see that Mistress MacLean was digesting that. She turned and began to pace as she mulled. ''Some of the women and older lasses could be assigned to see to the comfort of the children, freeing the rest to concentrate on their safety.''

''Their safety? That is the job of the men, my lady.''

''The men would be busy fighting off the invaders. I believe it wise to look to our own safety, Mistress.'' She turned. Paced some more. ''There are steps we could take. For one, the villagers could move their flocks closer to the castle, so that they can be herded within the walls if invaders are spotted in the hills."

The housekeeper thought a moment. "Do you think that wise, my lady?"

"Aye. Don't you see? That assures us of an unlimited supply of meat. Also, those harvesting crops in the fields could store some here in the abbey, to insure that the larder is well stocked. If we see to the food, warmth and shelter, our men can concentrate all their energies on holding back the enemy without fear of a long siege."

The housekeeper looked at Gwenellen with new respect. "I'll send Olnore to the village to speak with the women this very day."

"A fine idea." Gwenellen thought about the messages she had yet to carry to the survivors of the siege. This would afford her the perfect opportunity. "I would like to accompany her to the village."

"Aye, my lady." The housekeeper paused. "Can you think of anything else we might change?"

"There is one thing, though it has nothing to do with invaders." Gwenellen thought about Andrew's parting words. "I'd like to talk to you about the great hall."

"What's this?" Andrew stepped into the great hall and looked around in surprise. No fire burned on the hearth. There wasn't a single servant in sight.

Gwenellen paused in the doorway before hurrying

over to join him. "I persuaded Mistress MacLean that this room was too big and too drafty to suit the laird."

He shook his head in disbelief. "You're amazing. We're dining in the library?"

"Nay, my lord. Your housekeeper wouldn't hear of it. She said there wasn't a servant in your employ who would set foot in that place. But she did agree to serve a meal in the withdrawing room." She met his eyes. "Are you disappointed?"

"Not a bit. I still think you're amazing. And you didn't even have to resort to a spell." He studied her closely, sending heat flaring up her throat. "Or did you?"

"I had no need. Mistress MacLean was only too happy to please the laird of the abbey."

"Ah, well. You can always try a spell next time." He led the way from the great hall, then moved along beside her as they made their way to the withdrawing room.

She felt the warmth of his body as they walked. Felt the press of his hand on the small of her back as he guided her through the doorway. Why had she never been aware of such things before? How was it that a simple kiss between them should change so many things?

When they stepped into the smaller room, they were greeted by a cozy fire burning on the hearth, and a table set with snowy linens and fine crystal.

The housekeeper looked up from a sideboard groaning under the weight of heavy silver trays. "I hope this meets with your approval, my laird."

"It does indeed, Mistress MacLean. I must commend you. This is much more comfortable than the great hall."

Pleased, the older woman filled two goblets and offered them to the lord and his lady before going off to fetch the servants.

Andrew touched his goblet to Gwenellen's. "To you, my lady, for getting us out of that drafty hall and into this cozy room."

"You might not thank me when you realize how far the servants must carry the food, my lord. It could well be cold by the time it gets here."

"As long as I have you to look at, I'll not mind the passage of time." Now where had that come from? He'd vowed not to say or do anything that might lead to anything even remotely intimate. And here he was, in the first few moments with this woman, forgetting all his carefully-made plans.

There was just something about her that made it easy to forget the pain of the past, the uncertainty of the future.

He decided to keep their conversation business-like. "The lads had their first lessons with a sword today."

"How did they do?"

"Well enough. What they lacked in skill they more than made up in enthusiasm."

"Enthusiasm?" She wrinkled her nose in that funny way she had, and he couldn't seem to look away. In fact, he found himself enthralled by the tiny line of freckles that seemed to march across the bridge of her nose whenever she did that. "I can't imagine looking forward to doing battle."

"And I can't imagine spending my days stirring stew in a kettle."

That had Gwenellen laughing. "Nor I."

"That's right." He met her smile with one of his own. "You'd rather practice your magic, wouldn't you?"

"Aye. Speaking of magic, I went to the village today with Olnore."

"Why? It isn't market day."

"I had messages to take to some of the villagers. I spoke with Shepard about his duty to his granddaughter. And to Roland the crofter who owes two lambs to Melvina's son and his wife. And Charity's niece…"

He held up his hand, halting her words. "You admitted to these villagers that you spoke with their dead relatives?"

"Aye."

He bit back a smile. "How did they receive the news?"

"They were a bit…doubtful, at first. But when I

relayed all that the dead had told me, especially personal things which only the dead could know, I believe they were convinced of my claim.''

''And now they know you to be a witch?''

She nodded. ''I know this isn't easy, my lord. For you or for them. But since this is my responsibility as well as my gift, I am bound to see it through.''

His tone softened. ''That refreshing honesty is just one of the many things I find so appealing about you, Imp.''

The use of the unexpected nickname, spoken like an endearment in low, intimate tones, sent a shiver along her spine.

It took her a moment to find her voice. ''Has the messenger returned yet from Edinburgh?''

His smile faded. ''Nay. He's long overdue. I fear he may have fallen victim to a barbarian's sword.''

Sensing his tension, she lowered her voice. ''What will you do if your warriors don't return?''

''I'll face Fergus Logan with an army of old men and lads.''

''Are you so certain your enemy will return?''

Andrew's eyes narrowed. ''He'll return. If I don't ride to his fortress first.''

''But your father…''

He held up a hand to silence her protest. ''It is my father I am thinking of. As a warrior and his son, I owe it to his memory to demand justice. For now, I must bide my time and train the villagers to defend themselves. But know this. As soon as my warriors return, I intend to ride to the Logan fortress and face my enemy like a Highlander, instead of hiding behind the walls of an abbey like a coward."

"And your father's wishes mean nothing?"

"It's time for me to accept the fact that my father is dead. I'm the laird of Ross Abbey now, however reluctant I may be. And the decision must be mine alone."

"But there are things your father knows that are unknown to—"

At a commotion in the doorway they looked up as the housekeeper entered, following by a line of serving wenches.

Whatever Gwenellen had been about to say was swallowed back in disappointment. The opportunity to discuss this with any sense of calm or reason had vanished.

As Andrew began to lead her toward the table she shook her head. "Forgive me, my lord. But I am...feeling unwell. By your leave, I wish to be excused."

His eyes narrowed as he stopped to look at her, seeing the disapproval she couldn't hide. It was obvious that she had taken sides with his father against him in this matter. That only served to stiffen his resolve.

"By all means, my lady." His voice was as cool, as casual as though he were addressing one of the servants. "I'm sure that Mistress MacLean will send a tray to your chambers."

Gwenellen turned away, eager to escape.

When she was gone, he held out his goblet to a servant and drank, ignoring the little twinge of guilt. He'd be damned if he'd allow one annoying female to tell him what to do. Though she played a most convincing game, he was still only half persuaded that she was what she claimed to be. Only a fool would count on magic to decide the fate of an entire clan.

Now that he was laird of the Ross Clan, he had an obligation to see that his people not only survived, but also thrived. They could only do so by eliminating their enemy.

He drained his goblet and took his place at the table, watching in silence as the housekeeper filled his plate.

She looked up. "The villagers have taken the lady's advice, my laird."

"Advice?"

She nodded. "Already the women are busy weaving warm blankets, and sewing additional sleeping pallets. From now on the herds will be brought closer to the abbey, and the larder kept well-stocked."

"What is this, Mistress? What is this about?" Andrew's brows drew together in a frown.

"The lady Gwenellen suggested that there is much we can do to prepare for an attack by our enemies,

my laird. In truth, it gives us all a feeling of satisfaction to be working as diligently as our men.'' She
stepped back. ''Would you care for anything else,
my laird?''

''Nay, Mistress MacLean.'' He lifted a hand and
idly waved her aside. ''You and the servants may
leave now.''

''Leave? I don't understand.''

''I have no further need of you, Mistress MacLean.
You and the servants may retire to the refectory. And
you may as well take these trays with you and eat
while the food is still warm.''

''Aye, my laird.'' Struck speechless, the poor
woman managed to sputter a few words of command,
as she ushered the servants from the room.

When he was alone Andrew shoved aside his plate
and lifted his goblet, drinking deeply.

For a lifetime he'd known exactly who he was and
what he was about. But in the past few months his
life had taken so many strange turns. Sabrina. His
father. And now this…witch.

He deeply resented her intrusion into his life. He
didn't want to believe the things she claimed to do,
because that would only complicate things further.

Still…

There was just something about her that he
couldn't entirely dismiss. Since dropping out of the
sky and into his life, everything had begun to change.
The villagers had drawn together to help him in his

sorrow. The men and lads were working diligently to become warriors. And now, to learn that she'd even convinced the women to band together for the common good, had him feeling like a thoughtless, arrogant fool.

And try as he might, he found himself spending entirely too much time thinking about her. Trying not to vent his anger whenever she questioned his authority. Trying not to laugh at her clumsy attempts at spells. He clenched a hand at his side. And especially trying not to give in to the desperate desire to carry her off to his chambers and make wild, passionate love to her until his hunger was sated.

Chapter Eleven

Instead of going to her chambers, Gwenellen fled to the garden, to walk among the graves. At least here she could be assured of hearing the truth. Those who had crossed to the other side had no need to lie, or to cloak their words in half truths.

Not so the laird of Ross Abbey, it seemed. One minute he claimed to believe her when she told him about his father's words, the next he was making plans to do exactly what he'd been warned against.

He was the most infuriating man. With but a single word, he could make her heart flutter. With one kiss she could forget every promise she'd ever made to herself about mortals. And then, in the blink of an eye, his smile would turn to a scowl, his manner become cold and distant, and her poor heart splintered.

She tossed her head. It didn't matter. He didn't

matter. She didn't need the laird's approval. Nor had she come here seeking his smiles. His kisses.

A figure shimmered before her. The woman named Melvina hovered above her gravesite.

"I thank ye, my lady, for setting things right with my cousin and the serving wench who was blamed for my sin."

Gwenellen paused. "You're most welcome. It wasn't an easy thing to resolve. I'm not certain your cousin believed me at first."

"But ye've a way about ye. She may not have wanted to listen, but I know she took it to heart, for I'm at peace." The figure began to waver and blur. *"Bless ye, my lady. I can go to my rest now, assured that my debt is paid and my time in eternity blissful."*

While Gwenellen watched, the figure disappeared.

Shaken, she strolled on, glancing up at the sliver of moon in the darkened sky until she heard the now-familiar voice.

"Good even, lass. I see ye were able to set the record straight with Duncan's wife and the young servant who had been unfairly blamed for Melvina's crime."

"Aye, my lord." Gwenellen paused beside the older man's grave. It was always a jolt to see him looking so like the angry man who was now laird of Ross Abbey. "It does my heart good knowing Melvina is finally at peace and can at last enjoy her eternal rest."

"There've been others as well, eh lass?"

She nodded. "So far I've managed to persuade three people of their messages from the grave." Her voice lowered. "But I fear I'm failing you, my lord. Your son's heart seems to be hardening against me."

"There, now. Don't you think that. Andrew believes, lass. At least in his heart. But he's fighting it. It goes against everything he's ever learned as a warrior."

"Then why do you ask it of him? Why are you so insistent that he not lead an army against his enemy?"

"Because it's exactly what Fergus Logan wants, lass. He'd hoped that Andrew and his warriors would return from Edinburgh and immediately ride to the Logan fortress in search of the hostage. They would have been met with an army bent on massacre. What Fergus Logan couldn't have known was that Andrew would leave his warriors to guard the queen, and return home alone, thus needing time to train a new army."

"You make it sound as though your son's enemy knew everything about him."

"And so he did. Or at least he thought he did. Never underestimate the enemy, lass. Fergus Logan had a spy in our fortress."

Gwenellen sank down into the grass beside the grave. "Of course. Andrew wondered how his enemy knew when to attack. Is the spy here in the village?''

Morgan Ross shook his head. *''Evil prefers to remain with evil. The spy is now in the fortress of our enemy. But that is why Andrew must not go there. He needs to—''*

''I thought I'd find you here.'' Andrew's voice cut through the darkness.

Gwenellen looked up to see him looming over her. When she turned back, the figure of his father had faded from sight.

''Chatting with the spirits, are you?''

''With your father, as you well know.'' She got to her feet, smoothing down her skirts as she did. ''You were right about the timing of the attack, my lord. Fergus Logan had a spy in your midst. He knew when your father would be most vulnerable.''

''A spy.'' He studied her through narrowed eyes. ''Did my father give you a name?''

''Nay. I believe he was about to, but you came along and…'' She drew in a breath. ''I know you don't want to hear this, my lord, but your father warns again that you mustn't go to the fortress of Fergus Logan, for that is what Logan wants. Your enemy expected you to ride there immediately, not knowing that you returned without your warriors. For every day you hesitate, he will grow more uneasy. And that is to your advantage.''

"Do you pretend to know battle strategy now, witch?"

Witch. What had happened to the endearment he'd whispered earlier? She felt a quick, sharp pain around her heart and wondered that this cold, distant man could have such an effect on her.

"I know nothing of war. I know only what your father has told me."

"So you say." He continued to study her. "I wish I could believe. But it isn't easy to turn my back on everything I've always known. I was taught that once the dead were gone, all that remained were the memories."

"Memories are fine, for they remain with us and warm us all through our lives. But what of the soul, my lord? The spirit that burns so brightly in each of us, and sets us apart from every other creature? Can that spirit be so easily extinguished? Or is it like those stars up there, shining upon us even in the light of day, when they're no longer visible to the eye?"

"What a strange one you are." He glanced beyond her to his father's grave, then took her arm. "Walk with me."

As they moved along the grassy path she could feel the warmth of his touch through her sleeve and wondered that, even now, knowing he doubted her, she could be so moved by the mere touch of him.

Andrew found himself looking up at the heavens, and noting the winking of millions of stars. "I've spent all day with the villagers.'' His voice was hushed. Perhaps it was the darkness. Or perhaps it was that glint of silvery light overhead. Whatever the reason, he wanted to prolong their time here, away from the watchful eyes of those inside the abbey. ''I hope you don't object to walking here with me.''

Gwenellen's smile was back. ''I've seen more people in the few days I've been here at Ross Abbey than in my entire life, my lord. There are times when I find my head spinning from all the people talking at once. Not just the living, but those who have passed over as well. They speak to me in a chorus of voices. At times I crave the silence of this place.''

That brought a chuckle. ''We're alike, you and I, Imp. There are times when I want nothing more than to ride my steed up into the hills, so that the only thing I'll hear is the babbling of a Highland brook or the cry of a falcon.'' He looked around at the peaceful setting. ''After hearing your tales of your kingdom, I find myself wondering what it would be like to climb aboard a winged horse and lose myself among the clouds.''

Her smile bloomed. Was it his easy use of that name? Or was it the mere fact that he had sought her out for company?

''Oh, it's like no other feeling. To soar on a current of air, and then to find yourself hurtling toward the ground, only to pull up short and land ever-so-gently in a field of heather.''

He loved the way her eyes went all dreamy whenever she spoke about her home.

He paused and covered her hand with his. "You make it sound so…normal."

"It is, in the Mystical Kingdom." She felt the warmth of his touch all the way to her toes, and wondered that they didn't curl inside her boots. "I suppose normal is whatever we've grown accustomed to."

"I could grow accustomed to this." He allowed his hand to linger a moment longer, before turning to walk beside her once more.

She could feel the return of his restlessness. The sense that there were things he needed to do, other than a quiet walk in the garden.

"What troubles you, my lord?"

He shrugged. "A better question might be, what doesn't trouble me? As if my enemy is not enough, there is the safety of the villagers if he should attack. And then there is my father's wife." He looked over. "Did he…speak of her?"

Again she heard the hint of something in his tone. Something that caused a little tremor of disquiet, though she knew not why.

"He did not." She shook her head and saw the way his frown returned. "But if you'd like, I could seek him out on the morrow and ask."

"Nay." He seemed distinctly uneasy, and just as quickly changed the subject. "Mistress MacLean tells me you are helping the village women prepare for a possible attack.''

''I hope you don't mind, my lord.''

''Now how could I mind? Your suggestions were excellent. Especially about stocking the larder.'' He arched a brow. ''You'd best beware or I'll start to believe there's a clever mind hidden behind that pixie smile.''

''I wish I were clever.''

''Why?''

She shrugged. ''It seems to be what mortals admire.''

He thought about that a moment. ''I suppose we do. But I'm beginning to think there are other things to admire as well.''

''What things, my lord?''

He turned to stare at her. In the moonlight she caught a glint of something dark and dangerous in his eyes.

''Sweetness. Honesty. Purity of heart.'' He touched a hand to her cheek. Just a touch, but he felt the rush of heat and wondered that he wasn't burned by it. ''You fascinate me, Gwenellen Drummond.'' He framed her face with his hands and stared down into her eyes, feeling a tug of such desire, he could no longer deny it. ''You're unlike any woman I've ever known.'' He drew her close and marveled at the way her softness melted against him. ''And though

I know I haven't the right, I must kiss you.'' He lowered his face and covered her mouth with his.

Though he struggled to keep it light, the kiss was hot, hungry, hinting of a passion smoldering just beneath the surface, waiting to erupt.

Gwenellen could feel him in every part of her body. Her thighs were pressed to his; her breasts crushed against the wall of his chest.

Heat poured between them as he took the kiss deeper and she experienced another emotion. A strange sense of fear. Fear that this man had a power over her that no man ever had before. With but a single touch he had the power to set her on fire. To wipe her mind clear of every thought save one. She wanted more of this. More of him. More of everything he could give her.

He gripped her shoulders almost painfully as he dragged her closer and savaged her mouth. She could feel his heartbeat in her own chest. Could feel his breath mingle with hers.

She opened to him, inviting him to take. And he did. The hands that moved over her were almost bruising in their strength. The mouth moving on hers seemed to feed from her even while it drained her, until she was struggling for breath.

At her little gasp he seemed to realize his strength. His touch, his kiss gentled. That was her undoing. She leaned into him, loving the feel of his arms as they held her as tenderly as though she were a fragile doll. Her fingers clutched the front of his tunic, as she gave herself up to the pleasure. Such incredible pleasure. How had she lived so long without this potent male taste filling her lungs, her mind? Without this hard body fitting itself so easily against her softness?

Andrew was drowning in the taste of her. So sweet, so exotic, he could imagine himself in another world, floating on a cloud while making love to her. It was all he wanted. This woman. In his arms. In his bed. Now. Here.

Catching her by the shoulders he lifted his head and held her a little away. His breathing was as ragged as hers.

"I'd best get you back inside, before I do something we'll both regret."

She couldn't speak over the tightening in her throat. She held herself very straight, very still, struggling to gather the thoughts that had scattered the moment he'd first touched her.

Wordlessly he took her arm, guiding her along the now darkened path.

Where had the moon and stars gone? Without his lips on hers, it felt as if the whole world had gone dark.

Inside the abbey they nodded at passing servants, and continued up the stairs until they reached the door of her chambers.

Andrew bowed over her hand, but was careful not

to touch his lips to her flesh. The need would be back, making their parting impossible.

"Good night, my lady. Sleep well."

"And you, my lord."

Once inside she composed her features as she greeted her little maid. She barely listened as Olnore chatted about the household gossip while helping her into her nightdress.

When the servant was gone Gwenellen stepped onto the balcony and stared at the darkened sky, wondering if Andrew was looking at the same sky, and remembering their kiss.

Or had he already taken to his bed without giving her another thought?

"Oh, Father." Odd, that in times of trouble it was always her father to whom she turned. Perhaps because he was the only one who loved her without reservation. Her family had such high expectations, and she hated the fact that she'd never lived up to them. But her father loved her just the way she was, with all her faults. And they were too numerous to recall. Clumsy. Sometimes thoughtless. Always too eager.

"I'm so confused. I have these…strange feelings for the laird."

She felt a whisper of breeze beside her, and her father's voice. *"Love is a strange and mystical emotion, my daughter."*

"But how will I know if what I'm feeling is love?"

"Your heart will tell you. Trust your heart."

"I do trust my heart. It's Andrew I'm not sure of. What if I let myself love him, and he doesn't return my feelings? Will my heart be broken?"

"Hearts do break. And they also mend. Just remember, everything worth having, in your world and his, requires some risk. If you should return to the Mystical Kingdom without letting yourself explore these feelings, you may never know what love is. The choice is yours, my daughter. I know you will choose wisely."

"How can you be so sure of that, Father?"

Gwenellen felt the breeze lift her hair as it rushed past her. And then the night was calm and still.

But not so her heart. It was pounding as she went inside and lay on her pallet, mulling her father's words.

Her heart could be broken.

Dare she risk it on this aloof, complicated man?

Chapter Twelve

"That's it, lads." Andrew nodded his approval as the village men and boys divided into two teams, going through a mock attack and defense. The late afternoon was filled with the clang of blade to blade as they danced across the meadow.

At first their clumsy attempts at swordplay had been crude and awkward. But slowly they'd come to accept that this was not play, but survival. Now they boldly faced each other down, thrusting and parrying as though their very lives depended upon each movement.

Women and children had taken over many of the farming and herding chores, freeing their men to spend their time under the watchful eye of the laird, who'd proven himself a strong, resourceful leader.

While their days were spent in learning the skill of warriors, their nights had been spent polishing their weapons, until knives and swords had been honed to razor sharpness. Each morning they lined up with their weapons for an inspection by their laird. One reprimand from him would send a hopeful warrior to the wheel, to sharpen his blade yet again. One kind word had a villager beaming with unmistakable pride.

It was the same for the women. With Gwenellen leading the way, they had begun to harvest their crops, taking only what their families needed for the coming weeks, and storing the rest in the abbey larder.

Flocks of sheep now grazed just outside the abbey gates. The nearby hills were dotted with cattle, with women and children posted at the highest peaks to watch for strangers.

Seeing movement across the meadow, Andrew lifted his head to watch as Gwenellen and a group of village lasses made their way toward him. In their arms were baskets brimming with crops from the fields.

He lowered his sword and stood watching the sway of her hips as she drew near.

For days he'd busied himself from dawn to dusk, hoping to fill his mind with something besides the way she'd tasted when they'd kissed. Now, just seeing her had it all rushing back.

''Good day, my lord.'' Gwenellen smiled and balanced the basket at her hip.

"My lady." He couldn't seem to tear his gaze from her face, sun-burnished and slick with sheen.

Neither of them seemed to notice the men and women milling about, exchanging pleasantries. They had eyes only for one another.

She struggled not to let any emotion creep into her voice. "I've not seen you these past days."

He caught sight of the way her damp gown clung to her breasts, and felt his throat go dry. "I've had much that needed to be done."

"Mistress MacLean says you rarely take time to eat, and then only in your chambers, or with your men."

"Aye." It had been an effort to stay away from her, but he'd made a decision he believed was best for both of them. Now, seeing her flushed and happy in her work, he could feel his resolve wavering. "Perhaps I could take the time tonight." He saw the smile that lit her eyes and knew he couldn't resist any longer. "It would be good for the men to go home to their women. After all this hard work, they need a rest from it."

"Shall I tell Mistress MacLean that you'll be taking a meal below stairs?"

"Aye. Perhaps in the withdrawing room again." He paused just a beat. "Will you join me?"

Her smile was dazzling. "I'd be honored."

When she turned away he stayed where he was,

watching the way her gown hugged her backside
with each step.

He turned back to his warriors, eager for the day
to be done. "All right, lads. Show me what you can
do with those weapons."

"I saw the laird coming in from the meadow."
Olnore knelt beside the tub and poured water over
Gwenellen's hair until all the soap had been removed. "He said to tell you he would stop by your
chambers on his way below stairs."

Her mistress struggled to get up, sending water
sloshing over the rim of the tub. "How long ago was
that, Olnore?"

The girl laid a hand on her arm to still her movements. "Not long, my lady. You have plenty of time
to dress." She held up a blanket, wrapping her in it
as she stepped from the tub.

Forcing herself to relax, Gwenellen settled herself
at a dressing table while her maid dressed her hair.

While she worked Olnore chatted on about all the
fine things the men had been saying about the laird.
"Though he's impatient to face his enemy, I'm told
he's a most patient teacher. He never scolds the lads,
though 'tis said they forget from one day to the next
more than half of everything they've been taught.
But instead of beating them, as is his right as laird,
he simply goes through the lesson again."

Gwenellen gave a gasp. "He could beat them?"

The lass nodded. "Some lairds are cruel masters. I've heard that Fergus Logan once beat a young lad to death for forgetting to stoke the fire in his chambers."

Gwenellen couldn't hide the shudder that rippled through her. "What sort of mortal is he, that he could actually beat another to death?"

Olnore studied her reflection in the looking glass. What had started out as rumors and whispers about this sweet, tenderhearted stranger, had now been confirmed. She actually carried tales from the dead. Tales that could no longer be disputed, since they'd been confirmed by many in the village. But this was the first time she'd heard the lady speak about mortals as though she herself weren't one of them.

A witch then. But surely the kindest, sweetest of witches.

"Fergus Logan is a cruel man, my lady. The Highlands would be well rid of such as him. It's said he once attacked Lord Andrew when the two were young because the little laird's steed tossed him, causing him to tumble from a mountain peak and come to rest on Logan soil. To Fergus Logan that was reason enough to thrash the laird and leave him for dead."

Gwenellen clapped a hand over her mouth to silence her little cry. "How did Andrew survive, Olnore?"

"'Tis said he crawled for two nights, hiding by

day beneath the branches of low-hanging bushes, until he reached Ross land and was found by a crofter who took him in and sent for the old laird.''

Seeing her dismay, the little maid decided to say no more about the cruelties of men. ''What of the men in your land, my lady? Are they kind or cruel?''

Gwenellen gave a clear, tinkling laugh. ''There are no men in my land, Olnore.''

''No men, my lady?''

She shook her head. ''Only women and one very old troll.''

In the mirror she could see the maid's shocked look and quickly turned around to lay a hand over hers. ''My home is the Mystical Kingdom, Olnore. And though I'm not as gifted as the others in my family, what you've heard about me is true. I can speak to those who have passed from this world.''

Olnore sank to her knees, all the while staring into Gwenellen's eyes. ''Could you...'' She swallowed and tried again. ''Could you speak to my mum, my lady?''

''Is she buried in the village?''

The lass nodded.

''I'll go there with you one day soon and we'll have a visit.'' Seeing the little maid's eyes fill, she stood and embraced her. ''It will be a grand visit, for the two of you will have much to catch up on.'' She stepped back. ''Now I think it's time I got dressed.''

Olnore brushed away her tears and helped Gwen-

ellen into a gown of ruby velvet, then stepped back
to admire her handiwork. "The color suits you, my
lady. But then," she added with a smile, "everything
you wear seems to suit you." She held out a matching cloak of ruby velvet. "Let's see how this looks."

Gwenellen waved her away, eager for the evening
to begin. "I need nothing more, Olnore."

"But, my lady…"

"Go now. Wear it to the stables to visit Paine."
She gave the lass a hard, steady look. "You are
meeting him, aren't you?"

"Aye. Thank you, my lady. But I could never
wear something so fine." Cheeks flushed, the servant
dropped the cloak on a chaise before dancing across
the room. At the door she turned. "I almost forgot.
Somehow in today's training in the meadow the
laird's dirk was lost."

"The one given him by his mother?"

"Aye. The lads have agreed to begin hunting for
it at first light, for they all know what it means to
the laird." She hurried away, pulling the door shut
behind her.

Deep in thought, Gwenellen walked to the balcony
and stared at the distant meadow. She, too, knew
what that dirk meant to Andrew.

She could fetch it for him right now.

She could already imagine the pleasure in his eyes
when she handed it to him.

Lifting her arms wide she began to chant the ancient words. As the chanting ended she closed her eyes. ''Search along the meadow ground. What is lost must now be found. While upon this balcony, bring the jeweled dirk to—''

Before she could complete her command a flash of silver danced across the sky and seemed to be heading directly toward her. End over end the knife flew, its jeweled hilt catching the last rays of fading sunlight.

Gwenellen gave a laugh of pure delight at the knowledge that she had finally cast a spell that worked.

''Oh, come to me.'' She clapped her hands then reached out, but the knife danced high above her and looked as though it might sail clear over the abbey towers.

''Nay.'' Determined not to fail again she climbed up on the rail of the balcony and made a grab for the tantalizing knife.

In the next instant her feet slipped out from under her and she found herself falling. She reached out and made a desperate grab for the railing. Though her fingers were slippery, she managed to catch hold of the very edge.

Once again she found herself dangling high in the air, the result of a spell gone awry. But this time she knew if she fell, she wouldn't just break a few bones. There was a very good chance she wouldn't survive.

* * *

Andrew closed his door and started down the hall toward Gwenellen's chambers. Nothing could dim his high spirits. Not the loss of his dirk, nor the fact that he'd heard not a word from his warriors in Edinburgh. Not the ragtag army he was training, nor the fact that he would have to spend the rest of his life as a proper laird instead of living the carefree existence of a warrior. Right now the only thing that mattered was that he was going to spend the evening in the company of the most delightful woman he'd ever known. He had no doubt that all the cares of the day would soon pale next to her.

He was smiling as he knocked on the door to her chambers, then opened it.

"My lady." He stepped into the sitting chambers, noting the cozy fire burning on the hearth. Perhaps later they would return here, and sip a bit of ale.

The door to her sleeping chambers stood open. He could see that she wasn't inside. He stood in the middle of the room and tried to ignore the little wave of annoyance. He'd wanted, after all, to escort her down the stairs. In fact, he'd been as eager as a randy youth just to see her. Now he felt deflated, and more than a little out of sorts.

Why hadn't she waited for him? Had her maid forgotten to tell her that he would stop by her chambers? Or had she simply not cared enough to do as he bid?

He turned away and stormed across the room.

With his hand on the door he paused and looked over his shoulder. Had he heard her voice? Or had that been merely the call of a bird?

"My lady?" He turned, hoping to see her appear in the doorway of her sleeping chamber. Again he felt a wave of disappointment and was just turning back when he heard it again.

Not a bird. Gwenellen's voice, but sounding faint and very strange.

He crossed the room and entered her sleeping chamber, letting his gaze sweep the empty room.

"Imp? Where are you?"

"Here. Oh, help." The voice sounded from the balcony, but he could see no one there.

He stepped out onto the balcony and saw her fingers clinging to the very edge of the railing. When he rushed over and saw that tiny figure dangling above the hard, punishing paving stones of the courtyard hundreds of feet below, he felt his heart plummet.

"God in heaven."

At his muttered oath, Gwenellen felt her fingers slip just enough to lose her grasp. At the same moment his strong hands grasped her wrists, keeping her from falling to her death.

For the space of a heartbeat he merely held her. Then, slowly, gently, so as not to scrape her tender flesh, he was pulling her up, up, over the railing and into his arms.

For a moment, when she found herself once more on her feet, all she could do was close her eyes and cling to his strength. Oh, how good it felt to be held by him. She felt a sob well up in her throat and burst free.

"Here now, Imp." His words were muffled against her hair. "Don't cry."

"I'm…not…crying." She managed the words between sobs.

"Of course you're not." Because he needed to, he gathered her even closer, until he could assure himself that she was truly here. Truly safe. He rocked her like a child, until his heartbeat returned to near normal.

Then, because anger was easier to deal with than fear, he held her a little away and scowled. "What in heaven were you thinking? Was this another of your silly spells?"

Her eyes widened. Her head came up in that infuriating way she had, while her chin jutted and her lips quivered. "Silly spells?"

"Aye. That's what I said. Silly. Useless. Not only useless, but dangerous. You know better. What was it this time? Did you want to fly again? Or were you trying to balance along the balcony like one of those fool tightrope walkers in Edinburgh?"

She pushed free of his arms, eyes blazing. Now her fear was forgotten. In its place was anger as out-of-control as his. "I wasn't trying to fly, or to balance. I did it for you."

"For me? You're saying you tried to kill yourself for me?"

"For your dirk." She reached into the waist of her gown and slapped it into his hand before turning away to hide the tears that stung her lids. "Olnore told me you'd lost it in the meadow. I wanted to surprise you."

She flounced away and called over her shoulder. "Tell Mistress MacLean that I beg her pardon, but I've lost my appetite."

Before he could say a word she snatched up the ruby cloak and ran out of her chambers. Minutes later he stood on her balcony and watched the small figure running across the garden.

Even from this distance he was certain he could see the glitter of tears on her cheeks.

The sight of her tore at his heart, before he turned away, muttering every rich, ripe curse he could think of.

Chapter Thirteen

"Here you are, my laird." As Andrew stepped into the withdrawing room, the housekeeper caught sight of his angry countenance and blamed it on the missing dirk. The household was abuzz with the news. Everyone knew what it meant to him.

She glanced beyond him. "Where is the lady?"

"She is…taking the air in the garden."

"Ah. Well then, perhaps you'd care for some ale while you wait?"

"I'll have the ale, then you may serve the meal, Mistress. The lady seems to have lost her appetite."

"Very well, my laird." She handed him a goblet, then signaled for the servants to approach the table.

Andrew glanced around at the cozy fire, the small, perfect setting, and wished he were anywhere but here.

He took a seat and studied the salmon, poached to perfection. And the mutton stew, one of his favorites.

The biscuits were nicely browned, and soft, the way he liked them.

He knew he wouldn't be able to eat a bite. Guilt, self-disgust, loathing, lay like a boulder in his stomach. What had provoked him to heap ridicule on the one person who meant so much to him?

He moved the food around his plate, while the servants hovered, lifting the domed lid of one steaming tray after another for his inspection.

He drained his goblet, only to have it filled at once. The thought of taking the decanter of ale and finding a quiet place to sit and get properly drunk was most tempting.

Instead he cut a piece of salmon and chewed. It tasted like ashes in his mouth.

The housekeeper hovered. "How is your meal, my laird?"

He looked up. "Fine, Mistress. My compliments to the cook."

She beamed.

He took another bite and wondered how much longer he would be able to remain the object of so much attention. The table was practically ringed with servants, and all of them watching him. He felt like a beetle swimming in a pond, with frogs all around. Watching. Waiting.

Was this what it would be like for the rest of his life? Servants circling him, eager to do his bidding, while he had nothing more to do than grow old and fat and lazy?

He thought of his father and felt a twinge of guilt. Being laird of the clan hadn't changed Morgan Ross in any of those ways. He'd remained alert and active and thoroughly involved in the lives of his people. He'd visited their cottages, celebrated their marriages and the births of their bairns. Had helped his people bury their dead, and had seen to the safety of widows and orphans. And though the thought of going off to battle with his comrades still tantalized him, Morgan Ross had known that his place was here, with the people who depended upon him for their safety.

Andrew knew that he would have no trouble following the example of his father and becoming thoroughly involved in the lives of these good people. But for now, for this night, all the joy had gone out of it. And all because he'd hurt the one who had brought the sunlight into his life.

Aye, that's what she'd done. Brought warmth and joy and…excitement back into this sad place.

There was a blur of movement in the doorway and heads turned.

Gwenellen looked completely disheveled, her hair a riot of wind-tossed tangles, her cheeks red as apples. Her eyes still glittered, though from tears or defiance, Andrew couldn't tell.

He could have devoured her whole.

The housekeeper smiled. "You're back. Have you worked up an appetite now, my lady?"

"Nay." Gwenellen's gaze darted from the older woman to the stern-faced man seated at the table. After much agonizing she'd decided she wouldn't give him the pleasure of driving her away. She would show him he didn't matter in the least. "Aye. I believe the sight of all that food has just restored my appetite, Mistress MacLean. I think I could eat something after all."

"That's fine, my lady." The housekeeper turned to the servants, who picked up the silver trays and stood at attention.

Andrew shoved away from the table and held a chair for his guest. She refused to look at him as she sat, but she felt the brush of his fingers at her back. She ignored the little curls of pleasure that danced along her spine and busied herself accepting fish and meat and biscuits from the servants' trays.

The housekeeper was happily prattling. "So, you took a nice walk in the garden, my lady?"

"Aye." Gwenellen moved the food around her plate, wondering how she could manage to eat a single bite. She shouldn't have come here. She should have taken refuge in her chambers. But she'd had this terrible need to see Andrew, even though she knew he would be still angry and frowning.

"A good thing you returned before it grew too dark."

"Aye, Mistress, a good thing." She broke apart a biscuit and took a bite, then was forced to sip ale in order to swallow it over the lump in her throat. She chanced a quick look at Andrew's face. It was as she'd feared, darkened with a scowl. All because of her.

"More salmon, my laird?"

"Nay. I believe I've had sufficient."

"Cook will be distressed if you don't try her lamb, my laird."

He gritted his teeth as he helped himself to a generous portion. Now there was even more food to stare at. Food that would surely choke him if he tried to swallow a bite of it.

He darted a glance at Gwenellen's face at the same moment that she happened to look over at him.

Both looked down, staring hard at their plates.

He cleared his throat. "How…was the night air?"

"Cool." Was that her voice? She sounded like Jeremy. Aye. Like the croaking of a frog. The ridiculous thought had her biting the inside of her mouth to keep from grinning.

"At least you had your cloak."

"Aye." Another croak, and she quickly lifted a goblet to her mouth to cover the little laugh that bubbled up.

He was staring at her with an odd expression. "Your cloak amuses you?"

"Nay. Aye." She looked around at the circle of

servants watching in stony silence, and feared she would soon explode. "It's just…" A hiccup of laughter had her placing her palm over her mouth. "It's just that the garden was so busy tonight…"

"Busy?" He arched a brow.

"Voices, you see. Such a chorus of voices, I didn't have a moment to myself."

It occurred to her that, though the housekeeper and servants hadn't moved, their expressions had altered somewhat. A few mouths had opened in silent protest. Ah, well. What did she care? Half the village knew she could talk to spirits. What was the harm if the rest of them knew? Let them all know that she was an outsider who would never be like them. Let them cross themselves whenever she passed and whisper behind her back. She was weary of trying to pretend to be one of them. She was a witch. Not a very good one, but a witch nevertheless.

"Everyone shouting at me with a request, a favor, an apology as I passed their graves…"

"Speaking of apologies…" Andrew placed a hand over hers.

The current that shot between them was so shocking, they both drew back as though burned.

Except for the hiss and snap of the logs on the fire, there wasn't a sound in the room.

Andrew caught sight of the housekeeper and servants watching and listening with rapt attention.

Instead of her hand he closed his fingers around

the stem of his goblet and lifted it to his lips. "I'm truly sorry, my lady."

Her head came up. Her eyes widened. Was he actually lowering himself to apologize?

Then she, too, glanced at the servants before clenching her hands in her lap and saying softly, "Thank you for that."

He set down the goblet, wanting desperately to touch her. "It is I who thank you."

He picked up his fork. Managed a bite of mutton. Then dropped the fork with a clatter before turning to his housekeeper. "Mistress MacLean, you and the servants are dismissed. The lady and I wish to be alone."

"Aye, my laird." With a wave of her hand the housekeeper sent the servants to the sideboard, where they deposited their silver trays before taking their leave.

Until the door closed behind them, neither Andrew nor Gwenellen said a word.

When they were alone Andrew picked up his goblet and strode to the fireplace where he stared for long moments at the fire. At last he turned. Gwenellen was still sitting at the table, her food forgotten.

"What you did, my lady, retrieving my lost dirk, touched me deeply."

She kept her face averted. "I am happy I could be of some assistance, my lord."

"Don't do that." He drained his ale and tossed the

goblet down with such force, it shattered on the hearth.

Stunned, Gwenellen shoved away from the table and got to her feet, staring at him in alarm. "Now what have I done to anger you, my lord?"

"You're behaving like a fine proper lady."

She gripped the back of her chair. "That offends you, my lord?"

He swore and was across the room in quick strides, his hands closing around her upper arms until he nearly lifted her off her feet. "I am not your lord. And I much prefer my imp, to some fine proper lady."

Her mouth opened, but no words came out.

His tone lowered, though it was still rough with passion. "I see you laughing inwardly at some foolishness and I want to share it. I see you dashing around the abbey like a little whirlwind and I want to be there, racing right alongside you."

Again he felt the heat of her touch, but this time he was prepared for it. It poured between them until the very air seemed charged with it.

For the longest time they merely stared at each other. Suddenly he dragged her into his arms and pressed his mouth to her temple. "Gwenellen, my wonderful little imp. I can't bear that I made you weep."

"I didn't weep." Her eyes filled and hot tears spilled down her cheeks, dampening the front of his tunic. She wanted him to go on holding her like this forever. Was nearly overwhelmed by the fact that he'd opened his heart, his soul to her, with such vehemence. "I never weep."

"Of course you don't." He was kissing her. Her temple. The curve of her cheek. The corner of her mouth, where he tasted the salt of her tears. "You're too fine and sweet and wonderful to ever have a need for tears. But I hurt you. I was the cause of them, and for that I'll never be able to forgive myself."

"Nay, Andrew." She drew back to lift a hand to his mouth. "I've already forgiven. And forgotten. You mustn't punish yourself. I know I'm a burden…"

"Don't ever say that." His eyes were hot and fierce as he stopped her words with a quick kiss. He drew back just enough to look into her eyes. "You are the most remarkable woman I've ever known. And now, right this moment, I must kiss you again. Or go mad."

He drew her close and covered her mouth with a kiss that spoke of all the need, the hunger that he'd so long denied.

She answered with a hunger of her own that caught them both by surprise. With her arms around his neck she clung to him, thrilling to the passion, the heat, the need, that flowed between them.

"Oh, Andrew. I want…" She struggled to find the words. Did she have the right? She didn't know. Had no lessons in the ways of mortals. But she had to try. "I want you to love me." She nuzzled his mouth with hers. "As a mortal man loves a woman."

At her words he froze.

Needing to clear his head he pushed her a little away and took in deep draughts of air. "You don't know what you're saying."

"But I do. I want you, Andrew. And I think…at least I hope you want me."

"Of course I do. What you're offering is everything I've wanted. Dreamed of, from the time we first met. But think what you're doing, Imp."

She wound her arms around his neck and gave him a smile that would melt glaciers. "I love it when you call me imp. It's ever so much sweeter than my lady."

He groaned, wondering how he could find the strength to resist her. But one of them had to be strong. "Once we do this thing, there'll be no going back. You won't be the innocent on the morrow that you are this night. Think about that, Gwenellen."

"I don't want to think. I want you, Andrew." She pressed her mouth to his throat and heard his quick intake of breath. "I want this…this fluttery feeling that comes over me whenever you and I come together."

His hands tightened on her arms and he held her a little away, his eyes hot and fierce as they stared into hers. "What am I to do with you, Imp?"

"Love me, Andrew. Just love me."

His breath came out in a long, deep sigh. "God in heaven. How can I not?"

And then his mouth covered her in a kiss that nearly devoured her. When at last he drew away her lips formed a little pout.

"Again," she whispered.

He gave a dry laugh. "If I do, I won't be able to stop."

"How grand." Her smile was radiant. "I don't want you to stop."

"Nor do I. But sooner or later the servants will return." He gave her a dangerous smile. "And I'm in no mood to be interrupted by servants. We need to go somewhere away from the others." He skimmed his mouth over hers. "I suppose we could bar the door to your chambers or mine. But even then the servants will simply stand outside waiting to enter."

She gave him a sly smile. "I know a place where the servants will never bother us."

"Where?"

Her smile grew. "The old abbey library."

She saw him considering her suggestion before he cupped her face with his hand and kissed her soundly, lingering over her lips until he caught himself going under. It was so easy to fall under the spell of this woman.

Against her mouth he muttered, "You really are a

clever little imp. And if I don't get you out of here this minute, I'll never make it.'' He caught her hand. ''Follow my lead.''

As they stepped out into the hall they encountered the housekeeper who was poised with her hand lifted, just about to knock.

''Finished so soon, my laird?''

''Aye, Mistress.''

''Cook has made a tray of sweets, my laird.''

''Thank Cook, and send my apology. The lady and I have had our fill.''

''Will I send ale to your chambers, my laird?''

''That won't be necessary. Good night, Mistress MacLean.''

''Good night, my laird.'' She gave a light bow of her head, trying not to stare at their disheveled appearance, or to make too much of the fact that their breathing was overly shallow. Still, she gave a knowing smile at their retreating backs as she called, ''Sleep well, my laird. My lady.''

Chapter Fourteen

Andrew and Gwenellen moved quickly along the hall, acknowledging any servants they met with a simple nod. Neither of them spoke. Nor did they touch. But each was achingly aware of the other. Of the heat that seemed to shimmer and pulse in the very air between them. Of the furtive glances with each hurried footfall. Of the purposeful way they moved, desperate to reach their goal.

Finally they rounded a curve and stepped into the old section of the abbey. After following another hallway, they paused at the doorway to the library.

As Andrew shoved open the door, Gwenellen felt her heartbeat quicken at the thought of what they were about to do. Would he find her inexperience laughable? Would she be as clumsy in her lovemaking as she was in other areas of her life?

Then he turned and smiled, and her fears evaporated like the mist over the Enchanted Loch. This was what she wanted. What she desperately craved. To be held in this man's arms. To be loved. Woman to man.

"Afraid, Imp?" He gathered her close and brushed his lips over her temple.

"I was. But not now."

"And why is that?"

"What I feel is so strong, so right. As though we were meant to be together here. Do you understand?"

"I do." He nodded. "I was afraid, too." He smiled. "But not now." His hands moved along her back, causing the most amazing sensations to slide, like fire and ice, deep inside.

"You were afraid? Truly?" For some strange reason that admission made her heart feel incredibly light.

"Truly. You're so very special to me, Imp." He rained soft butterfly kisses across her upturned face. "So sweet. Untouched. Each time we've kissed, I've thought about a score of ways to love you. But always I was afraid. Afraid to spoil someone so unsullied by this world."

"And now?" She stared into his eyes as though searching for answers.

He tossed aside her cloak and ran his hands up her arms. "And now we're here together, and, right or wrong, I'll have my fill of you."

She shivered and gave a little laugh. "You make me sound like Cook's sweets."

"You're so much better." The look in his eyes was a mixture of teasing laughter and simmering desire. "Every time I see you I want to devour you."

He dragged her close and kissed her, lingering over her lips as though she were the sweetest confection. His hands were in her hair, drawing her head back while he kissed her until they were both breathless. And still it wasn't enough. He wanted to crawl inside her skin. To take her, hard and fast, like a barbarian. Instead, he held back, keeping his kisses gentle enough to allow her to relax and open to him.

Open she did. Her lips to his. Her body, straining toward his, with the most incredible rush of heat. And her heart, eager to accept the love he was offering.

Lost in the kiss, she reached out blindly, her hands clutching his waist. She had the sudden notion that her legs might fail her and she would slide bonelessly to the floor. His kisses had a way of doing that. Of making her weak, and turning her world on its head. Surely it was magic. A very special kind of mortal magic that only he possessed. Not that she cared, as long as he didn't stop doing what he was doing, for it was mesmerizing.

He brushed wet nibbling kisses down the smooth column of her throat.

She tried to push away while bursting into gales of laughter. "Andrew, that tickles."

"And this?" He drew her close and buried his mouth in the little hollow between her neck and shoulder.

Her laughter turned to a low moan of pleasure as he continued down her collarbone to her breast. Despite the barrier of her clothing her nipple hardened instantly at his touch.

She hadn't expected that quick tug of desire, or the liquid warmth deep inside that had her trembling with strange new needs.

"A moment, Andrew." She placed her palms against his chest. "I can't think."

He ran his hands lightly up her arms. "There's no need to think, Imp. Just feel."

"But I feel so…" She tried to put it into words, but all she could do was sigh. How could she possibly explain the way her body vibrated with such need, it had her shuddering.

He gave her a heart-stopping look. "Would you like me to stop?"

"Nay." Her hands fisted at the front of his tunic, holding him when he started to pull away.

Against her lips he muttered, "Praise heaven for that. I don't know what I'd do if you asked me to stop now." With a chuckle he wrapped her in a fierce embrace and covered her mouth with his.

He took the kiss deeper until their chests were heaving, hearts thundering.

When at last they came up for air, he reached for the buttons of her gown. His fingers fumbled and he swore. "Why must there be so many buttons on women's gowns?"

"I never thought of it before. Perhaps it's intended to preserve our virtue."

She saw his quick grin. "You don't think a few buttons will do it?"

She laughed, and the warmth of it trickled over him like warm honey. "Not when you're in such a mood as this. Shall I help you, my lord?"

"Allow me, my lady." Before she had time to realize what he planned, he tore the bodice in two and the gown slipped away, pooling at her feet.

"Andrew." Her eyes widened. "How will I explain this to Olnore?"

"You'll tell her that the buttons were much too small for your lover's hands."

"My lover?" Again that wide-eyed reaction, as she realized the implication. "You are, aren't you? Truly?"

"Truly." He reached for the ribbons of her chemise. With one tug the delicate fabric parted.

He slid it from her shoulders, all the while staring at her with a look that spoke more than words. She was so incredibly lovely, standing in the spill of moonlight from high, narrow windows above. The sight of her took his breath away.

"Oh, my beautiful Imp." The words were spoken with a sort of reverence.

Then those strong, warrior's hands were touching her. Moving along her body. The soft curve of her breasts. The narrow waist. The gentle flare of hips. His mouth followed the trail of fire started by his fingertips. With lips and tongue he kissed, caressed, worshiped, slowly driving her mad.

He was losing himself in her. Her scent, as fresh as wildflowers. Her sighs, whispering over his senses like the siren song of some exotic bird. Her skin. Pale as milk, and softer than the underside of a rose petal.

Each time she trembled at his touch he found himself more and more aroused until he thought he'd go mad from the need for her.

When she reached for his tunic he helped her until his clothes joined hers on the floor.

Now she was free to touch him as he was touching her. Her fingers moved tentatively across his face, over his shoulder, down his chest.

"You're so beautiful, Andrew."

"I've a warrior's body, covered with scars. It could hardly be called beautiful, Imp."

"But it is. You are. All that muscle. I've never before seen a man's body. It's so different. So…splendid." She trailed her hands across the flat planes of his stomach, then lower, until he moaned and covered her mouth in a savage kiss.

Her touch on his naked flesh was the most exquisite torture. He wanted, more than anything, to take what she offered here and now, and end this hard, driving need building inside. But he wanted so much more. He cautioned himself to go slowly. Now that he was free to indulge, he would have it all. He would take and give until they were both sated. A feast for one who'd been starving. A night undisturbed, to indulge in every kind of fantasy. This was what he craved for both of them. And they would have it, even if it took superhuman control.

Taking her hands he drew her down on the cloak and lay beside her, before covering her mouth in a searing kiss.

Gwenellen absorbed the quick rush of heat, then the slow, steady throb of need. She could actually feel her blood begin to pulse and flow like lava through her veins. When his lips left hers she made a sound of protest. But when his mouth began a lazy exploration of her body, she could do nothing more than sigh from the pure pleasure of it.

She lay steeped in the most amazing sensations. As though she had just discovered her own body through his touch. She'd never dreamed a man's hands could be so compelling. She could feel him in every pore. Could taste him on her lips. Could smell the distinct male musky scent of him deep in her lungs.

She felt beautiful. Desirable.

Andrew could feel her begin to relax in his arms, as trust replaced fear. Trust. More than desire, more than need, the knowledge that she trusted him had his heart swelling with love for her.

His kisses deepened. His touch became more impatient. Teasing. Arousing, until she moaned and clung, afraid that at any moment she would burn to ash from the heat building inside her.

He saw the look of surprise mingled with pleasure as he brought her to the first unexpected peak. Those wide innocent eyes going sightless. The lips pursed in a question. And then her hands fisted in the cloak as she rode the crest.

This was how he'd wanted her. Alive, vibrant, and aching with need for him. This was how he'd dreamed of her as he'd paced his chambers in the dark of the night, thinking of the beautiful creature who slept but a door away. His. Only his. His woman.

He could feel the need rising, threatening to take him over the edge. Once again he pushed it aside, wanted to give her more. So much more.

His kisses were no longer gentle, but demanding, drawing her in, taking her to a newer, darker place. A place of hot, slick flesh, and shallow breaths that couldn't quite fill lungs that were straining.

Gwenellen was reminded of the first time she'd seen him. There had been a darkness about this man that had been as exciting as it was frightening. Now she was joining him in his darkness. But instead of fear, she felt a ripple of excitement. She not only welcomed it, but reveled in it.

She could feel her flesh melting, her bones dissolving. Despite the lack of fire on the hearth she was burning with fever. A fever that had her breath growing more shallow with every minute; her heartbeat more thunderous.

The room was so still, the only thing she could hear was the sound of ragged breathing. Hers and his. Two hearts drummed in unison. The only thing she could see was Andrew. Those dark eyes narrowed on her with such fierce concentration. Those warm, clever lips that were curved in a mysterious smile as he looked into her eyes. Those strong warrior's hands that brought such pleasure.

Following his lead she touched him as he'd been touching her and was rewarded by his low growl that seemed more animal than human. He dragged her into his arms and kissed her, long and slow and deep, until he could feel her actually quivering with need.

''Andrew.'' A voice she barely recognized as her own sounded more like a whimper than a sigh.

He knew he could wait no longer. As he levered himself over her he felt her tense.

Against her mouth he whispered, "I'll try not to hurt you, Imp."

She smiled then. The sunlight that he craved, lighting all the darkness inside him. "I know you could never hurt me, Andrew."

Her trust in him was as erotic as her touch. He knew now there was no way to stop, or even to slow the crest sweeping them both up and over. The beast inside him was struggling to be set free. He was being carried along in a tide of unbelievable pleasure as she took him in deeper and began to move with him. Climb with him.

"My beloved Highland warrior." Her words were a whispered sigh as she wrapped herself around him and matched her strength to his.

She would make him hers. Only hers.

With hearts thundering, lungs straining, they began to climb, to soar, until they reached the highest peak. With a starburst of incredible sensations they stepped off the edge of a high, steep cliff.

And soared through the heavens.

"What's this?" They lay, still joined, while their breathing slowed and their heartbeats steadied. With his lips against her cheek he tasted the salt and lifted his head to touch a finger to the corner of her eye. "Tears, Imp?" His tone hardened as he started to push free. "I never meant to hurt you."

"Nay, Andrew." She drew him close and touched

a hand to his cheek. "You didn't hurt me. I don't know what caused these tears." She sounded mortified. "I never cry."

"Of course you don't." He was feeling far too tender at the moment to remind her of the tears she'd shed not more than an hour ago. He rolled to one side and drew her gently into his embrace, wrapping her cloak around them both. "You're too sunny to weep."

"I am?" She snuggled close, loving the feel of his strong arms around her.

He nodded. "Do you know, each time I look at you I see sunshine?" He tangled his fingers in her hair. "It's probably because of all this light that surrounds you like a halo."

"I've heard of halos. I'm no saint."

His grin was quick. "Aye. I'll attest to that. But there's an aura of bright colors that seem always to surround you."

She lifted a finger to his face and began tracing the outline of his lips. Such amazing lips. They brought such unbelievable pleasure. "What else do you see when you look at me?"

He turned slightly, staring into her eyes and wondering that, even now, the mere touch of her could be so arousing. "Are you hoping to unearth all my secrets now, Imp?"

"Aye. If I were one of my sisters, I could see for

myself. But since I haven't the gift of sight, tell me what you see, Andrew.''

He traced a finger over the curve of her brow, the outline of her mouth. "In your eyes I see truth. On your lips I hear only honesty. While others around me might mask their feelings to spare mine, you'll tell me what I need to hear, even if it isn't to my liking.''

"I thought that angered you.''

He chuckled. "It does. Nobody wants to hear unpleasant things. But I admire you for your honesty, Imp. Especially since I've made it so difficult for you to speak the truth.''

"You can be a bit…overbearing, my lord.''

"Overbearing?'' He folded his hands behind his head. "I'm a model of evenhandedness. A man of infinite patience.''

That had her laughing. "Aye. A paragon of virtue.''

His laughter faded. "I haven't always been kind to you, and for that I'm truly sorry. Earlier today I made you cry and…''

She sat up and touched a hand to his mouth. "Hush. You couldn't know why I'd attempted another spell.''

"But I assumed the worst.''

"It was no more than I deserved.'' She flushed. "I'm well aware that my spells haven't always been successful. As for you, Andrew, I've seen how hard you're working to ease the pain of the villagers. And I've heard from them about your many kindnesses. You may pretend to be a heartless warrior, but your people knew better. They wouldn't have asked you to be laird if they hadn't considered you worthy.''

''Oh, Imp.'' He drew her down and treated himself to a long, lingering kiss. ''You almost make me believe that I can do some good here.''

''You're needed here. Without your leadership, what would these good people do?''

Before she could say more he shot her a dangerous smile and ran hot, wet kisses down her throat. ''Why are we wasting time talking, when there are so many more…pleasurable things to do?''

At the spiral of heat she clutched his waist and gave a little gasp of pleasure. ''You mean we aren't finished? There's…more that women and mortal men can do?''

''Oh, my wonderful, delightful little Imp.'' He threw back his head and roared with delight. ''There's so much more.''

With a growl of pleasure he covered her mouth with his and proceeded to show her.

As moonlight spilled over them like liquid gold, they lost themselves in the wonder of their newly-discovered love.

Chapter Fifteen

Gwenellen lay very still, wondering what had awakened her from a sound sleep. It took a moment to recall where she was. Then it all came rushing back to her. The library in the old portion of the abbey. The love she had shared with Andrew.

It felt so good to be here with him. So right. As though everything in her life had been moving her toward this place, this man.

It wasn't just the joy, the passion, the pleasure they'd shared. It was this room. It was, she felt certain, an enchanted place. The spirits of the ones who had sought refuge here eons ago lingered still. She could feel their presence. Could sense their approval. It gave her great comfort.

Some time during the night Andrew had started a fire and carried her to the fur-covered chaise. There, warm and cozy, they had whispered words of love while indulging all their fantasies.

He had been an amazing lover. At times so easy and gentle with her, as though they had known each other for a lifetime. At other times their lovemaking had more resembled a sudden summer storm. All thunder and lightning and bursts of passion that caught them both by surprise, sending them into a frenzy of need.

She heard the sound of labored breathing and Andrew's muttered oath as, caught in the throes of a nightmare, he thrashed among the furs.

"Andrew." Alarmed, Gwenellen touched a hand to his shoulder and felt him flinch. She shook him gently. "My love, wake up."

He sat up suddenly, his hand going to his waist, as though to reach for his sword. Feeling his bare flesh, his eyes snapped open.

He stared blankly at the vision beside him, before he blinked and seemed to pull himself from a dark place in his mind. "Forgive me, Imp. I woke you."

"You were having a bad dream, Andrew."

"Aye." In the glow of embers his skin was slick with sweat; his eyes narrowed in thought.

"Would it help to tell me about it?"

Instead of a reply he walked to the fireplace and tossed a fresh log on the hot coals. Within minutes flames began licking at the bark.

She studied the way he looked in the firelight. Tall and proud, his profile so cold and stern it could have been carved from marble. She could see, by the hands clenched at his sides, that he was still struggling with his demons.

His words, when at last he spoke, were gruff, as though forced from a throat raw with grief. "I had a bitter argument with my father before I left for Edinburgh. Things were said in the heat of anger that can never be recalled."

"What things, Andrew?"

He returned to the chaise, but instead of sitting beside her, he knelt at her feet and caught her hands in his.

"I'll not speak of them, for they're too painful even now. But I thought, when I left, that I never wanted to see him again. I can't help thinking that my wish was the cause of all that's happened here."

Gwenellen squeezed his hands tightly. "You must never think that, Andrew. You weren't responsible for what happened to your father."

"How do you know that? I wished it, didn't I? And now my wish has been granted." He shoved a hand roughly through the hair that had fallen over his forehead.

She closed a hand over his, feeling the spill of dark hair over their joined fingers. "Your guilt will do nothing but add to your burden." She slid her hand to his cheek. "If you are seeking someone to blame, then look to your enemy."

Seeing that he was about to protest further, she touched a finger to his lips and stared deeply into his eyes, as though daring him to argue. "Your father bears no resentment toward you. In our conversations he has expressed only love."

Andrew sighed. "If only he could speak to me. But I suppose I must be content with the fact that he can speak to you."

"Then you don't mind if I continue conversing with your father?"

"I welcome it. In fact, since I'm being completely truthful…" He caught a wisp of her hair and twirled it around and around his finger, studying the look in her eyes. "…I must admit that I'm more than a little jealous of your ability to speak with my father."

"You can speak to him, as well, Andrew."

"And you believe he will hear me?"

"Aye. I know he will. But he is unable to make a reply except through me." She leaned closer, brushing a kiss over his forehead. "There's no need to regret the words left unspoken between you. Speak to him of all the things that are in your heart, my love. Your father will hear you. And your own heart will be lighter for it."

He linked his fingers with hers, then looked into her eyes. "How did you get so wise, Imp?"

She shook her head. "I'm not wise. But I know that your father wouldn't want his only son to suffer so."

"Has he told you that?"

"Not in so many words. But he has spoken of his

love for you. And of his desire to keep you safe from the snare of his enemy.''

''Then I suppose I must be content with that.'' He pressed a kiss to her palm before folding her fingers over it, as though to hold it.

The gesture was so sweet and unexpected from this tough warrior, she felt a quick tug at her heart.

She lifted the edge of the fur. ''You must be freezing. Come here, my love, and I'll warm you.''

His eyes crinkled with laughter. ''Don't you know that you have only to touch me and I'm warm?'' He lay beside her and gathered her into his arms. Against her temple he whispered, ''And now, lying with you, I'm on fire.''

He ran a hand down her back, then slowly up her side, until he encountered the soft swell of her breast. As his thumbs teased, his mouth covered hers in a kiss so hot it nearly seared them both.

Against her mouth he muttered, ''See what you do to me?''

She chuckled, but the sound soon turned into a moan of pleasure. ''And all along I thought it was you who brought this heat, my lord.''

''It's the two of us together, love.'' As he indulged his passion, he marveled at the way she made him feel. Strong. Proud. And happier than he could ever recall. Perhaps she truly had healed his heart.

At first he'd felt merely a fierce need to protect this funny, sweet, strange little witch from herself.

After all, someone had to take care of her when her failed spells were constantly leading her into danger. But if he were honest with himself he'd admit that the greatest danger was to his own heart. He could no longer deny the fact that he was hopelessly in love. And not just in love with any woman, but with a witch, who had a habit of propelling herself into dangerous, deadly situations.

He would have to be vigilant in order to save her from herself. For he couldn't bear it if any harm should come to her.

And then, as their kisses became more demanding, and their need more demanding, all thought scattered as he once more lost himself in the pleasure of this wondrous new love.

"My love." Gwenellen awoke to find Andrew propped up on one elbow beside her, staring at her with such intensity, she found herself blushing. "What are you doing?"

"Watching you sleep." His lips curved into a smile. "Did you know that you wrinkle your nose every time the wind blows down the chimney?"

She shoved aside a tangle of furs and started to sit up. "I do not."

He wrapped his arms around her and held her a little away. "You do. And it's simply delightful to watch."

She avoided his eyes while tracing a finger over the mat of hair at his chest. "What else do I do?"

"Your lips purse. As though being kissed by a lover in your sleep."

She gave him that pixie smile. "Perhaps I was dreaming of someone."

"Give me his name, my lady, and he'll answer to my sword."

Her eyes widened. "You're jealous?"

"Aye. I want no other man to taste the sweetness that I've enjoyed this night."

"Not even an imaginary lover who visits only in my dreams?"

"Imp." He dragged her close and savaged her mouth. "I know you're teasing me, but I'd be jealous of even a man in your dreams. I want you to dream of only me."

As his hands moved over her she tried to resist. "Andrew. You know where this will lead."

"Aye, my love. To the same place we've been all through the night."

"But the sun is already upon us. If we don't soon hasten to our chambers, we'll be forced to face Mistress MacLean and the servants."

He chuckled against her throat, sending heat spiraling all the way to her core. "I'll worry about them later. For now, all I can think about is you, my love. Have pity on me, for I've been watching you, and wanting you, since before the dawn."

Whatever protest she'd been about to make was forgotten as he took her on a wild, reckless ride to paradise.

"Andrew." Gwenellen gave his shoulder a none-too-gentle shake until his eyes opened. "It's as I feared. Look." She pointed to the sunlight streaming through the narrow windows above them. "The sun is already high in the sky. The entire household must be wondering where we have gone."

"Let them wonder." He seemed completely unconcerned as he drew her down for a lingering kiss.

"But Mistress MacLean…"

"Is merely the keeper of my household. I am still master of Ross Abbey."

"But she'll know. As will all the servants."

"Let them, my love. I care not if the villagers, or for that matter, everyone in the Highlands know of our love." He plunged his fingers into her hair and kissed her again, long and slow and deep. When at last they moved apart he studied her eyes. "Are you troubled by this, Imp?"

She lifted her shoulders in a helpless gesture. "I know little of your world, Andrew. How will the servants react?"

"They'll whisper, of course. But none will speak aloud of the laird and his lady."

"Oh." She crossed the room and picked up her

gown, studying the torn bodice. "What will Olnore say when she sees this?"

"She'll say nothing, my sweet. And she'll see that it's properly mended before it's returned to you."

As she began to slip into her clothes he lay watching her. Seeing the smile on his lips, she paused. "Now what are you doing?"

"The same thing I was doing while you slept." The look he gave her had her heart hitching. "Watching you. And enjoying the vision very much."

"Aren't you going to dress, Andrew?"

"I'd planned on it. But now..." In one smooth motion he tossed aside the fur throw and crossed to her side. "Now I think I must taste heaven one more time before we part."

His eyes were hot and fierce as he slowly undressed her and carried her to the chaise. Without a word they came together with all the force of a Highland storm.

"Good morrow, my laird. My lady." Mistress MacLean paused on her way to the great hall and struggled not to stare.

The laird's tunic was wrinkled, his plaid tossed carelessly over one arm. A growth of stubble darkened his cheeks and chin. His hair was mussed.

At least the lady was properly covered from head

to toe by a hooded cloak. But a glance at her face showed high color riding over her cheeks.

The entire abbey had been in an uproar over the fact that the laird and lady had been absent from their chambers for the entire night. But where could they have gone to evade the staff?

"I see you were taking the air."

"Nay. We were here, Mistress. In the old abbey library."

"The old…" The housekeeper crossed herself. "'Tis a fearsome place even in daylight, but after dark…" Her words trailed off as she caught herself about to lecture the laird.

She turned to Gwenellen. "The servant Olnore was looking for you, my lady. I'll send her along to your chambers."

"Thank you, Mistress." Gwenellen started up the stairs, followed by Andrew.

The housekeeper's voice stopped them. "Will I have Cook prepare a meal, my laird?"

He glanced over his shoulder. "Aye. The lady and I will break our fast in the withdrawing room."

"Very good, my laird."

Andrew caught up with Gwenellen and took her hand in his. When they paused outside her chambers he leaned close to whisper, "Perhaps I could come in. Just for a moment."

She covered her mouth to stifle a giggle. "Not

even one moment, for I know where that would lead.''

''I didn't hear you complain earlier.''

''Nor would I again. But you heard Mistress MacLean. Olnore will be right along.''

''We could bar the door.''

''We could.'' She framed his face with her hands and kissed him full on the mouth. When he started to draw her closer she stepped back, evading his arms. ''I don't know about you, Andrew, but I'm going to wash and dress in clean clothes before I go below stairs to face the servants. I hope you'll do the same.''

''Imp…''

She stepped away and closed the door in his face.

As she started across the room she heard the door open and his voice, low and teasing. ''One moment alone and I could change your mind.''

''I've no doubt of that, my lord.'' She was laughing as she heard the little servant call out a greeting behind him before entering the chambers.

Andrew wisely took his leave.

''Here you are, my lady.'' Olnore, seeing the cloak, smiled. ''So. You and the laird were out riding. I should have known. Here, my lady. Let me help you with that.''

As she removed the hooded cloak, the little servant caught sight of Gwenellen's torn gown. ''Oh, my lady. Did you fall in the brambles?''

"Nay, Olnore." Gwenellen knew her face was flaming, but telling anything less than the truth was impossible for her.

She tossed aside her gown and turned away to wash in the basin, grateful when the servant began to chatter away about her most recent walk in the garden with Paine.

"He held my hand, my lady. And later he took me to the stable to see the new foal."

"Oh, Olnore." Gwenellen clapped her hands in delight. "A new foal. What color is it?"

"Color?" The servant's cheeks reddened. "It…was dark in the stables, my lady. I took no notice of the animal's color."

"Was it standing?"

"I…know not."

Gwenellen could see the betraying flush, and felt an instant kinship with this lass.

She lowered her voice. "So. You stayed the night in the stable?"

"Aye, my lady." Olnore stared at a spot on the floor.

"Was it grand?"

The girl's head came up. She saw the light of understanding in Gwenellen's eyes and knew that the rumors about the laird and lady had been true. "It was a fine, grand night."

"As was mine."

For long moments the two young women shared

a knowing silence. Then they hurried through the rest of their morning routine.

When a knock sounded on the door, the servant hurried over to admit Andrew, who had eyes only for Gwenellen.

With her hair gleaming from a good brushing, dressed in a fine new gown of palest pink satin, she looked every bit a high-born lady.

As they stepped from her chambers he offered his arm. "Are you hungry, my love?"

"I suppose I could eat something. Are you hungry, Andrew?"

"I am." He gave her a long, considering look. "Though it isn't food I'm hungry for."

She chuckled. "You're impossible, my lord."

"And you're so beautiful, you take my breath away, Imp." He paused at the bottom of the stairs and placed a hand over hers. "My day spent with the villagers will seem endless, until I can lie with you tonight."

As they made their way to break their fast he felt a lightness around his heart that had never been there before. It was as though the morning sun had burned away all the mist. A mist that had long clouded his vision. Now it had lifted, leaving him dazzled.

This woman was his sunlight. His moonlight. His starlight.

He wanted to bask forever in the delicious warmth of her.

Chapter Sixteen

"My compliments to Cook, Mistress." Andrew pushed away from the table. "The night air is warm, my lady. Will you walk with me?"

"I'd like that." Gwenellen was eager to join him.

As they took their leave of the great hall, the servants were smiling and bowing.

Everyone seemed to be basking in the glow of the laird's warmth. The staff at Ross Abbey whispered about the change in their master. Whatever tension had lingered after his feud with his father seemed to have slipped away. The village lads who trained in the meadow discovered a new patience in their teacher. And each night, Gwenellen seemed to peel away another layer of Andrew's armor, revealing not only a tender lover, but a man concerned with every aspect of the difficult life of a Highlander.

"Do you miss the excitement of Edinburgh?"

Gwenellen paused in the grassy path as they enjoyed an evening stroll in the gardens.

"Nay. My heart has always been here in the Highlands." He walked with her to a stone bench and settled himself beside her. "Here we have long been isolated from life in Edinburgh, and the pomp that surrounds the Throne. That can work to our advantage at times, making it difficult for invaders to reach our fortresses. But it can also work against us."

"In what way?"

"The queen requires an army of trusted soldiers. Most are recruited from among the Highlands, because our loyalty is unquestioned. But when our enemies invade, it is often impossible for our warriors to arrive in time to be of any use."

Gwenellen studied his stern profile. Now that she'd come to know this man, she understood that it wasn't anger, but concern for his people, that drove him. "You believe that Fergus Logan will attack before your warriors can reach us?"

He looked away. His silence spoke more than words.

She touched a hand to his arm. "Do you think the villagers are ready to fight like warriors?"

He turned and gave her a tired smile. "If a firm resolve could repel invaders, the people of the village would have no fear, for I have never met more determined fighters. But how are farmers and crofters to defend themselves against some of the most brutal swordsmen in all of Scotland?''

''If you fear for them, wouldn't you be better off to flee?''

''Where would we go? This is the land of our fathers.''

''But at least you would be alive, until you could train enough warriors to take back your land.''

''There would be nothing left to take back. Do you think Fergus Logan will simply help himself to our crops and flocks, and leave? When he returns to his fortress, he'll leave behind fallow fields, poisoned lochs, and barren countryside. And woe to any innocents he encounters along the way. The man is a brute and a bully. He has a need to fulfill a bloodlust. For too long now he has savaged his neighbors.'' Andrew's voice lowered with passion. ''He took something precious from me. I want him to answer for that.''

She shivered at the depth of his fury. ''Even if it means your death?''

He nodded. ''It matters not as long as I die with Logan's blood on my sword.''

He got to his feet and paced restlessly, while she watched. At long last he paused beside her, and closed a hand over hers.

His voice lowered to an intimate whisper. ''This talk of doom and gloom resolves nothing. Come, my love, and lie with me. And we'll speak of happy things.''

Happy things. If only, Gwenellen thought as they climbed the stairs, they could always be this happy. But the threat of attack hung over them like a pall. It was never far from their minds. And, she knew, it robbed Andrew of precious sleep. She'd heard him tossing and turning, and often watched in silence as he stood on the balcony of his chambers, staring into the night.

Forcing a brightness to her tone, she entered his chambers and tossed aside her cloak. ''Have I told you about the time Jeremy and I were picking rose-berries, and...'' Her words stilled as he walked up behind her and drew her back against him.

While his mouth moved slowly along the smooth column of her throat, his hands rested just beneath the fullness of her breasts. She couldn't control the tremors as his clever hands and mouth began to work their magic.

''Andrew, my story...''

''Will have to wait, love.'' He picked her up and carried her to his bed. ''For I need you. Desper-ately.''

They took each other in a frenzy.

Gwenellen awoke to the sound of men's voices in Andrew's sitting chamber. At first she thought to dis-miss them. Servants, no doubt, reporting something to their master. But as she lay in the darkness she could hear the urgency in Andrew's voice, and in the ones who answered.

Then there was only silence as a door closed and footsteps sounded in the hallways.

Moments later she saw Andrew's darkened silhouette as he crossed the room and stepped onto the balcony.

She tossed aside the furs and padded to his side.

He draped an arm around her shoulders and drew her close, then looked once more at the darkened hills. "I'm sorry I woke you, Imp."

"You know I can't sleep when you're not beside me."

He nodded absently. "I know." He took in a deep breath. "I must dress now, love. And so must you."

As he started away she tugged on his arm. "What is it, Andrew? What's wrong?"

He slipped into his tunic and hose before strapping on his scabbard. "I've had lads hidden in the hills, with orders to watch and listen."

"For Logan's men?"

He nodded. "I'm told that many men are on the move in the Highlands to the north of us."

"Logan's warriors?"

"Aye."

Her heart gave a little hitch of fear. "How soon will they be here?"

He tucked his sword in the scabbard, then tossed

the length of plaid over his shoulder. "Late on the morrow. They have no need to surprise us. They know that without my warriors, we have no chance to survive."

He said it so simply, she felt a chill along her spine. "And yet you'll stay and face them, knowing it means death?"

"We've talked about this, love. You know I must." With a tired smile he turned and framed her face with his hands. "Go now and dress. I've already sent word to Olnore what you will need."

"But…"

"Go." He kissed her. A quick, distracted kiss before stepping from his room.

Gwenellen hurried to her own chambers and found Olnore already there, an assortment of garments spread across the bed.

Gwenellen studied the heavy wool gown and hooded traveling cloak. "What is all this?"

The maid seemed as bewildered as her mistress. "I was told to prepare you for a journey, my lady. I know nothing more. Come now and we'll…"

Instead of changing her clothes, Gwenellen turned and raced down the stairs, unmindful of the fact that she was still in her nightdress. At the bottom of the stairs she found Andrew talking to the housekeeper.

When he saw her, his head came up sharply, and he signaled the housekeeper to leave.

Gwenellen remained on the lower stair, so that her

eyes were level with his. "Olnore said I'm to dress for a journey. Why, Andrew?"

He paused before her. "One of the lads who'd been posted in the hills knows every dip and hollow in this land. I would trust him with my life, or my most precious possession."

"I don't understand."

He placed a finger to her lips. "I sent him to the stables to tell Lloyd to saddle a horse for you."

She was shaking her head. "I have no need of a horse."

"The lad will accompany you to your kingdom."

She stiffened her spine. "I'm not leaving here, Andrew. I'll not leave you now."

"Shhh." He placed a finger on her lips to still her protest, and even that light touch had heat pulsing between them. "You have no choice, Imp. I am laird. And you will do as your laird commands."

"I won't." Tears stung her eyes and she blinked hard, ashamed to let him see her weakness.

He saw her tears and muttered an oath. He couldn't bear to see her cry. But this was not the time for weakness. He needed to be strong. Not only for himself and his people, but for her. "Understand something, my lady." His tone hardened, as did his formal use of her title. "You are here at my pleasure. And you have brought me great pleasure. But now I must concentrate all my energy on the battle to come. I cannot allow any distraction."

She struggled to keep the pain from her voice, though each word was an effort. "Are you saying I was nothing more than a...pleasant distraction?"

He heard the approach of horses and carts, as the villagers arrived to prepare for battle. Though he longed to drag her into his arms and kiss away her tears, there was no time.

No time.

He thought of the hurtful words he'd hurled in anger at his father. Words that could never be called back. The time for kind words had passed, and would never be given him again. And so this time he must choose his words carefully.

"You have been more to me than I ever dreamed, my lady. But now I must join my people to do battle with my enemy. It will bring me much comfort to know that you are in your Mystical Kingdom, where you will be safe, and carefree, and happy forever, far from this hell. That is where you belong. Not here."

Stung, she couldn't seem to wrap her mind around what she was hearing. "You can't mean this."

His tone hardened. "It's time for you to accept the fact that the idyll is over. I have no time for witches, my lady, no matter how sweet and charming. As you yourself told me from my father's lips, my duty lies with my people."

With a slight bow, he stepped back, breaking contact.

Gwenellen stood paralyzed as he strode out the

door to join his men. Then, blinded by a mist of tears, she turned and raced up the stairs.

"Where do you go, my lady?" Olnore slipped the coarse woolen gown over Gwenellen's head and helped her with her hose and kid boots.

"The laird has ordered me to return to my home in the Mystical Kingdom." Gwenellen sat at the dressing table while her little maid brushed her hair. "But I have no intention of going."

"My lady." Olnore stared at her reflection in the looking glass, her eyes as wide as saucers. "No one may defy the laird."

"What will he do? Have me flogged?"

"Nay, my lady. But he can have you tied to your horse and taken away in shame. Would you force him to do such a thing at this time, while he is facing such danger?"

Gwenellen closed her eyes. "Is there no way to defy him?"

"No way that I know of. Only a laird's family may challenge his word."

"Family." She opened her eyes. "Did you know Lord Andrew's mother, Olnore?"

"Nay, my lady." The little maid fastened the heavy curls with a jeweled comb. "She died before I was born."

Gwenellen stood, smoothing down her skirts with nervous, jerky movements. Each minute brought her closer to leaving, and she could see no way to avoid it. "And what of the old lord's second wife?"

"The lady Sabrina?" Olnore's tone hardened. "Her hair was as black as a raven's wing. Her body lush and perfect. I'm told she spent hours each day with her servants, until she was satisfied with every aspect of her hair and gown. She was the object of many men's lust, for she was a great beauty."

Gwenellen's hands stilled. "A beauty? She was young?"

"No older than you, my lady."

That fact shouldn't have startled Gwenellen, for she'd seen the magnificent gowns. Still, she'd pictured a woman closer to the old laird's age. "How long were she and Andrew's father wed?"

"Not long, my lady. No more than a fortnight."

Gwenellen's head came up sharply. "And Lord Andrew was gone to Edinburgh no more than a fortnight."

The little servant nodded. "He took his leave of the castle as soon as his father and the lady Sabrina began to speak their vows in the chapel. He didn't even take time to join in the wedding feast. Of course," Olnore added, "who could blame him, when the lady was betrothed to him before she wed his father."

Seeing the shock in Gwenellen's eyes she clapped a hand to her mouth. "Forgive me, my lady. I thought you knew. It was common knowledge here in the abbey.''

"I suppose everything the laird does is…common knowledge." She struggled to keep her voice carefully bland. "No wonder he and his father became bitter foes. He must have loved the Lady Sabrina very much."

"No more than…" Olnore swallowed back what she'd been about to say and held out the hooded cloak. "You will have need of this on your journey, my lady."

Carefully schooling her features, Gwenellen nodded. "Aye, thank you." As she drew it around her she caught the young maid in a fierce hug. "Goodbye, Olnore."

"Safe journey, my lady. I…deeply regret saying anything that caused you pain."

"You spoke the truth, Olnore. And for that, I should be grateful. I shall miss you."

"And I shall miss you, my lady."

Gwenellen waited until she heard the door to her chambers close. Then, with tears stinging her eyes, she walked to the balcony and stared out at the lovely green fields, and the distant, forested hills.

"Oh, Gram." Her voice was filled with pain. "How could I have been so foolish?" She pressed a hand to her mouth and turned away, wallowing in misery.

After all her grand pronouncements that she would

never do as her sisters had done and lose her heart to a Highland laird, she had done just that. And not just with any mortal. She'd lost her heart to a man who loved another.

"Nay." She wiped away her tears. "I've lost neither my heart nor my mind. Nor will I."

As she marched across the room she took a deep breath, willing herself to let go of the desire to weep. There was no harm done. Except to her poor heart. And that would heal. In a lifetime or two.

She knew now what drove Lord Andrew Ross. Though it was true that he sought to avenge the death of his father, there was something much more compelling that had him eager to build an army and stand up to his enemy.

She understood also why his father had gone to such great lengths to prevent his son from having his revenge.

Both men still loved the Lady Sabrina.

Gwenellen had been brought here merely as a bridge between the two.

Chapter Seventeen

The scene was one of frantic activity, as the men massed on the meadow, presenting their weapons for the laird's inspection, and the women and girls herded sheep inside the abbey walls and drove pony carts laden with whatever household goods they could manage.

Poor Mistress MacLean was rushing about trying to get an entire village settled inside the walls of one very crowded abbey.

Babies were crying. Sheep bawling. Men shouting. Servants dashing about, offering help wherever it was needed.

Gwenellen could hear the noise and confusion slipping away as she made her way along the darkened hall of the old section of the abbey. By the time she stepped into the library, there was only silence.

What a shame, she thought, that this wonderful old room would go unused by the servants and villagers, because of a foolish fear of those who had passed before them. Did mortals really believe the spirits of the dead would bring them harm? Didn't they realize that these good souls wanted only the best for their loved ones left behind?

She paused, feeling as she always did the sense of peace that came whenever she was in the presence of the spirits. A peace that wrapped itself around her like a warm shawl.

"I know I cannot stay here." Her voice was hushed, out of deference to this holy place. "The village lad is even now awaiting me in the courtyard, to accompany me back to my home. But I thank you for the sanctuary you offered me in this room. I will never forget it. Or the holy women who dwell here."

As she started to turn away her eye was drawn to the same high shelf where she'd first seen the strange, luminous book. It was there again, shining like a beacon in the shadows.

"How I would love to uncover your secrets. Alas, my flying spells have failed me too often to risk it yet again. Your secrets will remain hidden within the pages until someone wiser than I stumbles upon this place."

She turned away and started out the door. Just then there was a terrible crash. When she turned back, the book was lying on the floor, radiating more light than a score of candles.

She stepped cautiously closer, and realized the

pages were turning by themselves. Kneeling, she watched in fascination until the movement ceased and the book lay open. Because the pages appeared to be fragile, she didn't touch them as she leaned close and began to read the ancient words.

They seemed so familiar to her. Some were words she'd used in her own failed spells. Others were words she'd heard but had never spoken aloud. She stumbled over them as she struggled to speak each word.

When she finished, a strange silver mist began swirling around her. She scrambled to her feet, watching as the mist rose higher, wrapping around her waist, her shoulders, her head. Soon it formed a thick cloud that completely filled the room.

She felt no fear. She sensed that this cloud would cause her no harm. And as she breathed in the mist, she felt light as air.

There was a great rush of wind, dispelling the cloud. When Gwenellen looked around she was no longer in the abbey, but flying high above it. Then she was passing over the meadow, where Andrew and the village lads were forming their first line of defense. Sunlight glinted off their swords and knives and farm implements.

"So. I am meant to be here in the thick of battle. So be it." She folded her hands over her breasts, and lifted her face to the sky, ready to accept her fate.

Instead of lowering to the ground, she soared even

higher. So high the men far below took no more notice of her than they would of a bird.

The hem of her gown brushed against treetops as she floated over a Highland forest that formed a boundary between Ross and Logan lands. Once she cleared the forest, she looked down to see a long column of Highlanders, some on horseback, more on foot, headed along a grassy path that would take them directly to the meadow where Andrew and the others waited.

At the very head of the column were a man and woman, each astride magnificent horses.

Gwenellen peered down at them. The man was fair of hair, broad of shoulder. He sat his horse with ease, with a pride of bearing that spoke not of a man going to battle, but rather of one riding to glory. He chatted easily with the woman. The hood of her ermine cloak had been tossed back, revealing sleek black hair that spilled down her back. From Olnore's description, this could only be the Lady Sabrina, for she was a stunning beauty. But this was no captive, bound and forced against her will to watch the destruction of a lover. She tossed back her head and laughed at something said by the warrior. Then, while Gwenellen watched from above, the woman leaned close and touched her hand to the man's shoulder. He, in turn, cupped her face and kissed her.

For a moment, as they rounded a curve in the mountainous trail, the couple was hidden from the view of his men. Gwenellen felt herself dropping lower, until she could hear the words spoken between them.

"…badly misjudged Andrew." The woman kept her hand on the man's shoulder. "I was certain that famous temper of his would bring him to a quick end at your fortress."

The man shrugged. "Perhaps it's as I thought, and without an army of warriors beside him, the man is simply a coward."

"You'd be wise not to miscalculate, my love. His temper is legend. As are his courage and skill on the field of battle."

"Then perhaps your charms aren't as potent as you thought, my love. You did tell me he would be so enraged he would come after you even before he put his father in the ground."

"Aye. I misjudged him. No matter. By the end of this day, you will control all the land in these Highlands, as well as the people, who will have no choice but to swear allegiance to you."

"And to my bride." He chuckled. "Let the queen try to ignore us then. You and I will be a force to be reckoned with in Edinburgh."

Gwenellen felt herself suddenly lifting high above the tree line as the rest of his warriors came into view. And though she hovered in plain sight, no one looked up or took any notice, so intent were they upon the day that loomed before them.

She was lifted higher into the sky, until she could see both Logan's army and Andrew's. There would be ten or more men to every one of Andrew's. And while the village lads stood quietly awaiting their fate in the meadow, Gwenellen studied the razor-sharp blades of the swords belonging to Fergus Logan's army of warriors.

A shiver passed through her, and she lifted her face to the heavens with a feeling of helplessness. "What is the good of giving me this gift, if I have no way of using it? What am I to do with this new-found ability to fly?"

As if in reply she was whisked across the sky and dropped to the grass of the meadow with such speed, all she could do was lie very still and wait for the world to stop spinning.

She looked up as a sea of faces swam into her line of vision. And then all the faces faded but one. All she could see was Andrew, eyes narrowed, mouth twisted into a tight line of fury.

"I gave you an order, and you dared to disobey me?"

"I had every intention of doing as you asked, my lord. But I…" She glanced around at the others who were watching and listening in silence. "I wanted to visit the old abbey before I left. It holds precious memories."

He turned to the men and lads. "Return to your positions and watch for any sign of the enemy."

As the men dispersed, he reached out a hand to help her to her feet. Even that brief contact had her trembling, and she wondered that even now, knowing he loved another, she could feel this way.

His tone was tight with control. But anger was there, just below the surface. "You attempted another flying spell to evade my orders."

"I didn't know it was a spell. You recall the book I was seeking that first time you found me in the library?"

How could he forget? His poor heart had nearly stopped at the sight of her clinging to the very top shelf. He said nothing as he continued staring at her.

She took in a deep breath and started talking faster, afraid that in his present temper he might simply turn away and ignore what she had to say. "As I was taking my leave of the place, the book fell to the floor and the pages began turning. When they stopped, I read aloud the words, and the next thing I knew I was flying high in the sky."

He fixed her with a look. "And you expect me to believe that none of this had to do with my order to leave?"

"I didn't want to leave you. Nor do I want to now. But I'd had every intention of doing as you ordered. Andrew, you must believe me. There are forces here. Forces beyond our control. The holy women, your father…"

"Cannot fight my battle for me. Nor can you, my

lady. We will die this day. But we will die like warriors." His voice lowered to a fierce whisper. "But I'll not have you joining us in the carnage." He pointed toward the abbey. "You will leave me now. I must join my men. And you must obey your laird and return to the safety of your kingdom."

He turned away and started across the meadow.

"There's more, Andrew. I heard them talking."

He continued walking, and she had to run to keep up with his long strides.

"It's as your father said. This was all a trap, meant to lure you to Fergus Logan's fortress. His army is twice the size of yours. Once he has disposed of you and your men, he intends to claim your land and force your people to swear allegiance to him, in order to force the queen to acknowledge him."

He paused. "Do you think I don't know this? Logan has always been jealous of the bond between our clan and the queen. It is the reason why he, and his father before him, coveted our land and our warriors. He foolishly believes that with enough land and subjects, he will win the favor of his monarch. In the past we were able to turn away his overtures to war. But this time is different. He killed my father. Has taken as hostage my father's bride. Honor demands that we stand and fight." He turned away. "We waste precious time. Go now, my lady. Before it is too late."

She shook her head. "The Lady Sabrina is not Logan's hostage, Andrew."

Though he kept his back to her, she saw the way his head came up sharply.

"I heard him call her his wife."

He did turn then. The look in his eyes was frightening to see. "He forced her into marriage?"

Gwenellen shrank from his fury. If she'd had any doubt about his feelings for his father's widow, they were now gone. His hands were clenched into fists. His entire body seemed to stiffen with repressed rage.

"From what I observed, the decision was mutually agreed upon." She turned away. "I leave you now, Andrew."

He caught her arm and spun her around. "Are you telling me that she is not his captive, but his willing partner in this?"

When Gwenellen said nothing Andrew gave a curt nod of his head. "It's as I'd suspected. She was the spy in our camp. She used me, and then my father, to further Logan's ambition."

Gwenellen could feel tears stinging her eyes. This time, she told herself, they weren't tears of sorrow, but of anger. She lifted her head, determined to get through this with as much dignity as possible. "Now you know why your father fought so hard to keep you from running off to rescue her. I suppose this was also why he was so determined to keep you from learning the truth. He knew you were still in love with her, and he wanted to spare your poor heart from yet another blow.''

''Is that what you think?'' He took a step closer. ''I can see that you've been gossiping with the servants, my lady. They would know, of course, that my father and I had harsh words before his wedding. But they wouldn't know what we fought about.''

''I should think that was plain enough.''

''Nay. They only think they know. In truth, I had learned that Sabrina had used me to get to my father. I warned him, but he was so besotted by her, he refused to listen.''

At a shout from his men he looked over.

A long column of warriors could be seen at the top of a distant meadow. The size of the army sent a ripple of fear among the villagers.

Andrew gave a hiss of impatience as he closed his fingers around her upper arm and drew her close. ''I must join my men now. But before you leave me, I want you to know that with you I had finally found true happiness. And for that I will be eternally grateful. Now go, Imp. And know this. I do not fear death, now that I've tasted your love. Knowing that you're safe in the Mystical Kingdom will make my dying easier.''

He brushed her lips with a quick, hard kiss.

And then he strode off across the meadow, the jeweled hilt of his sword glinting in the sunlight.

Gwenellen knew that she'd never loved him as much as she did in that moment. She knew, too, that she would carry the image of this proud, courageous warrior in her heart forever.

Chapter Eighteen

"Oh, my lady." Mistress MacLean stood in the courtyard wringing her hands. "Where have you been? I've had servants searching the entire abbey for you." She lowered her voice to a whisper. "I even went to the old abbey library, thinking you might be there."

"That was very brave of you, Mistress." Gwenellen studied the woman's flushed face. "Did you see anything…unusual there?"

"Nay, my lady. It was merely dark and dusty."

"There was no book on the floor? Nothing glowing in the darkness?"

The housekeeper looked at her as though she were daft. "I saw nothing out of place, my lady. Now, as sad as it is for me to say this, you must do as the laird ordered and take your leave of Ross Abbey."

"Aye. In a moment." Gwenellen glanced toward the garden. "I would bid the old laird goodbye."

The housekeeper shot a look at the village lad, who stood holding the reins of two horses. Before she could argue Gwenellen had caught up her skirts and was racing toward the graves.

The housekeeper started after her. "Please, my lady. The laird has said…" Mistress MacLean's words trailed off as she saw Gwenellen pause beside the old laird's grave and hold out her hands, as though greeting someone.

The older woman shrank back as she heard Gwenellen's voice.

"Oh, my laird. At last." Her tone became accusing. "Where have you been?"

Morgan Ross brushed a kiss over her cheek and squeezed her outstretched hands. *"I've been resting, lass. It takes a great deal of energy to reach across our two worlds. I knew I had to save my strength for this day."*

"Right now Andrew is in the meadow, awaiting the arrival of Fergus Logan's army. An army that outnumbers his ten to one."

"I know that, lass. Andrew makes me so proud. He's the most fearless warrior I've ever known. Braver even than I was at his age."

"But he's going to die. As are all his men. Is there nothing we can do to save him?"

The old laird scratched his chin, as though thinking aloud. *"'Twould take superhuman powers to de-*

*feat an army of that size. Now if someone could fig-
ure out how to make Andrew's men fly..."*

Her head came up. "Fly? What good would that
do?"

*"What good would it do, you ask? Think about it,
lass. Logan's swordsmen would thrust with their
blades, only to find their opponents leaping out of
the way, over their heads, and dropping behind them
to attack. 'Twould be hard to defeat such an enemy.
Especially since there are those who would be ter-
rified after witnessing such amazing feats of magic."*
He chuckled. *"I fear many of Logan's brave warriors might flee in terror before facing such...
gifted opponents."*

"Then you believe there's a chance?"

*"I do, lass. Of course, it would take powerful
magic to make an entire village of men fly."* He
winked. *"Do ye know anyone with such power, who
just might have as much courage as my son?"*

Gwenellen thought about it a moment before nodding her head. "I might know such a person. Though
she's never before had any luck with her spells."

"That's my lass." He gave her a dazzling smile.

She stepped closer and threw her arms around his
neck. "Wish me luck, my laird."

Against her cheek he whispered, *"Luck has nothing to do with it, lass. All ye need is faith in ye'rself."*

When she stepped back, she could feel a soft,
misty dampness on her cheek.

She turned and began to run. "Mistress Mac-Lean."

The housekeeper stepped from her place of concealment, fighting to school her features. The poor lass was addled. There was no other explanation for what she'd witnessed. Standing at a gravesite, speaking in excited tones to no one, and then throwing her arms out, as if embracing the air. "It's time you did as the laird commanded, and took your leave of this place, my lady. For the sight of all this death and destruction has been too much for you."

"There's no time, Mistress." Gwenellen's mind was awhirl with plans. "I want you to summon the women to the courtyard with every bucket and basin and tub they can carry."

"Whatever for?"

"Just do it, Mistress." Gwenellen caught up her skirts and started toward the old section of the abbey. "I'll be right back. There's something I need to fetch."

"My laird." One of the lads shouted to Andrew, who stood in the midst of the village men.

"Aye. What is it?"

"There. Look, my laird."

Andrew turned, and could do nothing more than gape at the sight that greeted him. Gwenellen was running across the meadow, with the village women and lasses dancing close behind. Sunlight glinted off the things they held in their hands.

"What the devil?" Muttering a string of rich, ripe oaths, Andrew strode forward. "You would dare to defy me a second time, woman?"

"Aye, my lord." She paused a moment to catch her breath. "I had no choice."

"No choice?" He pointed to the line of warriors drawing close. "Soon enough, you'll have no life. Is this what you want for yourself and these helpless women?"

"They're not helpless, Andrew. Nor are you. Look." She held out the book.

While he stared in astonishment, the pages began flipping, one after another, until they suddenly stopped.

"What is this trickery…?"

"It's magic, Andrew." She touched a finger to the page. "Now gather your men around me."

"And why would I do that?"

She smiled. Though her lips trembled slightly, it was from exertion, rather than from fear. A sense of calm had descended upon her the moment she'd agreed to accept the challenge offered by the old laird. "I spoke with your father, and he showed me the way to defeat the enemy. Now I will share it with all of you. Together we can win, even against these incredible odds."

* * *

"Look, Fergus." Sabrina pointed to the figures gathered in the meadow. "Andrew Ross is so desperate, he even has the village women prepared to do battle."

Behind her the warriors broke into gales of laughter. As they drew closer and caught sight of the weapons, their laughter grew more raucous.

"Look at that. Buckets," shouted a grizzled old warrior.

"Aye. And basins," called a muscled youth.

"Farm implements," sneered a bearded giant.

Fergus Logan turned in the saddle and cupped his hands to his mouth. "Do those peasants think to stop us with such as these?"

That brought another round of laughter as the warriors unsheathed their swords and removed small, sharp dirks from boots and waistbands.

As they formed a solid wall of bodies and began the final march, their laughter faded. Their faces reflected the seriousness of what they were about to do. Though they didn't relish taking on women and old men, they would do the bidding of their laird. And they would, as day turned into evening, turn this meadow into a field of blood.

Andrew stood at the head of his ragtag army of men and lads, old women and lasses. He studied the line of warriors facing them. From this distance he could see the smirks on the faces of Fergus Logan and the stunning woman mounted beside him, who rode at the head of the army.

Surely, Andrew thought, he'd lost his mind. What else could explain the fact that he was exposing an entire village of good people to such a fate? They deserved better than this. But here he was, trusting their safety to a beguiling but muzzy-minded witch, who had never once managed a spell that would work. They might all end up floating in a loch. Or falling down some terrible, endless pit. Still, he had nothing better to offer them. The worst that would happen was that they would all die this day on the field of battle as they'd originally feared. Surely that was better than being enslaved by a monster like Fergus Logan.

He straightened his spine.

Desperate times called for desperate measures.

Gwenellen set the book down in a patch of heather before walking to his side and closing her hand in his. "Believe, Andrew."

"I'll try. But if I should die this day, Imp, there is something you should know. I really…"

Seeing a signal pass between Logan and his warriors, she shook her head. "There's no time, my lord. It begins."

Andrew used one arm to shove Gwenellen behind him. Then he faced his enemy. "Advance, Fergus Logan, and taste my sword. Or do you intend to hide behind your warriors?"

"I've no need to hide." Logan held out his hand to the woman seated on the horse beside his.

With a smile Sabrina placed her hand on his sleeve.

Logan's voice chilled. His smile faded. "The lady Sabrina and I are here to be entertained by my men."

At a signal from him his army let out a fierce roar, guaranteed to freeze the hearts of their enemies as they raced toward the villagers, swords at the ready. For their part the villagers stood in complete silence, awaiting a sign from their leader.

Andrew waited until the first swordsman was upon him before giving a shrill whistle.

Gwenellen lifted her arms, chanting the words from the book. There was a sound, as though a great rush of wind, and Andrew, along with the entire company of villagers was lifted over the heads of their attackers.

For a full minute there was a stunned silence from their opponents. Then, as Logan's men recovered their wits, they began screaming and shouting in fear.

"Witchcraft," someone called.

"Aye. 'Tis the work of the devil." A bearded warrior crossed himself and dropped to his knees in terror. At that very moment one of the village women sailed past him and knocked him senseless with her bucket, which was weighted with water.

Several village lads used their farm implements

like clubs, knocking warriors to the ground, before sailing out of reach.

A tall warrior managed to grasp Olnore's foot as she flew over his head. At her cries a cluster of women swooped at him brandishing basins of sand which they tossed in his eyes. While he cursed and blinked, they pulled Olnore free and drifted out of reach.

A cluster of Logan's warriors banded together and began tossing their knives at passing lads, hoping to bring them down. One of the lads, Paine, let out a howl, and began dropping to the ground. Before the warriors could grab him he was snatched up by Andrew, who handed him over to Lloyd.

"Carry him out of harm's way and see to his wound," he called before returning to the battle.

He turned in time to see Gwenellen sailing to the aid of Mistress MacLean, whose skirts had been snagged by the branches of a tree. As he aided in freeing her he muttered, "One of the pitfalls of flying, I suppose."

"Aye." The housekeeper giggled. "Though I must say I can't quite believe what I'm doing."

"Nor I," he admitted before turning away.

Logan sat astride his horse, watching the scene of chaos unfolding before him. The smile of victory had long ago been wiped from his lips.

His army was in shambles. Men were dropping to their knees in fear. Others were tossing aside their weapons and fleeing to the nearby forest, with shouts of witchcraft and devilment on their lips. Even the bravest among them, who had fought in the cruelest of battles, were afraid for their lives, for this was a new kind of enemy, and they had no idea how to defend themselves.

He turned to his most trusted warrior. "This is madness. Call back our army." To Sabrina he shouted, "We must join those who are fleeing, else we will fall under this witch's spell."

Sabrina had just taken up her reins when Fergus Logan saw the golden-haired witch rushing to the assistance of a village wench who had fallen to the ground.

Seeing his chance, he nudged his steed into a gallop and reached down, scooping up Gwenellen.

"Nay. Release me." Though she scratched and bit and struggled, she was no match for this man's strength.

In the blink of an eye he pulled his knife from his waist and pressed it against her throat.

His voice carried over the meadow, to the place where Andrew was just dispatching the last of the enemy warriors. "Andrew Ross. You will toss aside your own weapon and order your people to do the same, before kneeling in the grass, or the woman dies."

Andrew looked up to see Gwenellen in his enemy's arms. With a sense of horror he noted the knife at her throat, and the thin line of blood already staining the bodice of her gown.

The sight of it had his own blood freezing in his veins as he threw down his sword.

One by one, as the villagers saw what was happening to Gwenellen, they tossed aside their buckets and basins, their tubs and farm implements before floating to earth and dropping to their knees in the grass.

In quick strides Andrew made his way to where Fergus Logan sat astride his mount. "Release the woman, Logan."

Fergus threw back his head and laughed. A cruel, chilling sound that sent fear through the hearts of all who heard it. "Aye. I'll release the woman. When it pleases me." His voice hardened. "But first you will taste my justice, for I have long awaited this day."

He thrust his sword with such strength the tip passed through the flesh of Andrew's shoulder, sending him staggering backward, where he dropped to his knees in the grass.

Gwenellen's cry of horror pierced the silence.

With teeth clenched against the agony, Andrew pulled the weapon free, causing a river of blood to spill from the gaping wound. He was in too much pain and shock to do more than let the bloody sword drop from his nerveless fingers as he struggled to his feet.

Logan laughed again. A shrill, frightening sound

of madness that was echoed by Sabrina, who seemed completely unmoved by the bloodshed.

His words were equally frightening. "Now, Andrew Ross, before I'm through with you and this woman, you'll rue the day you ever heard the name Fergus Logan."

Chapter Nineteen

The villagers, who had been so jubilant scant minutes before, now went eerily silent as they watched the horrifying scene unfolding before them.

All their lives they had heard tales about the monster, Fergus Logan, and his cruelty toward anyone who dared to defy him. They had no doubt he would enjoy killing the young woman who had caused his humiliation. Especially if her death should bring pain to his sworn enemy. And then he would complete the cruel torture of their laird until he joined Gwenellen in death.

Andrew swayed, determined to remain standing before his enemy. He pressed a hand to the wound. Blood spilled through his fingers and ran down his arm.

A boiling, impotent rage seethed within him. "Your war is not with this woman."

"Nay. But I have the sense that she means something to you.'' Fergus watched Andrew closely as he tightened his grasp on Gwenellen and pressed the razor-sharp blade to her throat until she cried out. Seeing the flare of nostrils, and the quick flash of quiet rage in his opponent's eyes, he threw back his head and roared. ''You needn't say a word, Andrew Ross. Your face tells me all I need to know.''

He turned to the haughty woman beside him. ''How quickly he changes allegiance, my love. It would seem the reason he didn't come seeking your release is because he has lost his heart to another.''

''Only because she bewitched him. Look at her. How could any man lose his heart to the likes of her?'' Sabrina tossed her head. ''Not that I care about his foolish heart. Perhaps when you've finished with him, you should cut it out. It would make a fine feast for forest creatures. But before you kill him, I want him to kneel before me.''

''As you wish, my love.'' Logan turned a feral smile on Andrew. ''A pity about your choice in women. That one…'' He nodded toward Sabrina. ''…cared nothing about you or your father. You were both merely pawns in our little game. And this one…'' He grabbed a handful of Gwenellen's hair and tugged her head back sharply, causing even more blood to spill from the cut along her throat. His voice rose, so that everyone in the meadow could hear him. ''This one is going to die slowly before your eyes, so that you will see and understand the wrath of Fergus Logan. After the witch and your laird are dead, you will be given the choice of kneeling and swearing allegiance to me, or joining them this day in death. Now, Andrew Ross, you will kneel to my woman and to me.''

Instead of doing as he commanded, Andrew stood tall, his voice causing all heads to turn toward him. ''I'll not kneel to a coward.''

Logan's eyes narrowed with sudden fury. ''You dare to call me a coward, when you are the one standing here with neither weapon nor army?''

''Only a coward would take out his vengeance on a helpless woman. As for me, I need no army. Nor do I need a weapon. If you were a true warrior, you could prove it by ordering your army to step back and allow us to fight man to man, with nothing but our fists, until only one is left standing.''

''I need prove nothing, Andrew Ross. I am already the victor in this battle. And to the victor belongs the spoils.''

Andrew could feel his strength ebbing, and was desperate to goad his enemy into a fight before it was too late. Perhaps it was already too late for him, but a distraction might save Gwenellen's life. ''There has been no victory here, because you refuse to fight.'' He could see his enemy considering. To drive home his point he added, ''Unless you're such a coward you're even afraid to face a wounded man who has no weapons.''

"I have no fear. Of you or of any man." Logan turned to a hulking warrior and thrust Gwenellen into his arms. "Hold firmly to the woman and see that she doesn't try any more of her witchcraft."

To his men he shouted, "You will stand back until I've vanquished my foe. Then, any of these peasants who refuse to kneel and swear allegiance to me are to be killed at once." He turned to Andrew with a chilling smile. "Know this. As soon as your death is accomplished, your woman will be passed among my men for their pleasure. Before they have finished with her, she will beg to join you in death."

He leaned over and cupped Sabrina's chin in his hand, pressing a kiss to her mouth. "This won't take long, my love."

"A moment." Sabrina took a ribbon from her hair and tied it around his arm, then gave him a dazzling smile. "Remember that before you end his life, Andrew Ross must kneel to me. It will bring me much pleasure."

"I'll not forget." Logan slid from the saddle and stood a moment to study his opponent. Pointing to the blood-soaked ground at Andrew's feet he gave a laugh. "You could save yourself a great deal of pain, and spare me the effort of exerting myself, if you would simply kneel now, before it's too late."

"And miss the satisfaction of planting my fist in your face?" Andrew stood even taller. "I make you this promise. Never will I bend my knee to you."

"Then I'll have to be satisfied with your bloody body prone before me." Fergus pulled a knife from his waist and sprang.

The crowd gasped, and many of his own men were heard muttering that it wasn't a fair fight, for the agreement had been to fight with fists, not weapons.

Andrew was able to dodge the attack, but just barely. As he sidestepped, the blade of the knife caught his arm, adding another layer to his pain. He twisted back and closed his hand around Logan's wrist, squeezing until the knife slipped to the ground.

"Now, Fergus, despite my wounds, we're evenly matched."

"Why, you..." Angered that he'd lost his weapon, Logan brought his knee to Andrew's groin. With a grunt of pain Andrew dropped to the ground and sucked in several quick breaths, struggling to clear his vision.

Out of the corner of his eye he saw Logan poised to kick. He caught the booted foot and tugged, causing Logan to land on his back. Like a cat Logan twisted free and rolled aside, evading Andrew's hands as he made a grab for him.

When the two men regained their footing and faced each other, Logan was clutching the bloody sword, which he'd snatched from the grass.

Andrew eyed him warily. With each movement he was losing more blood. Soon, he knew, his body would simply fail him. "I see you're incapable of fighting with honor. Are you so afraid of my fists that even now you must resort to weapons?''

"Honor is for fools and dead men, Ross. I'll use whatever I must to defeat you. And defeat you I shall. Do you know why?''

Andrew began to circle slowly, waiting for an opportunity to spring.

Fergus kept him in his line of vision. ''The queen has long favored your clan, Ross, while choosing to ignore my offer of counsel. I wonder how long she can ignore me when she learns that her precious Highlander was too weak to defend his own land and people? When she learns that I am now laird of lairds? I wager that Sabrina and I will be given a royal welcome in Edinburgh, and your warriors will be replaced by mine.'' He chuckled. ''I will become the power behind the Throne.''

"Is that what this is about?'' Andrew paused, his head swimming. ''It isn't just my land you covet, but the power of the Throne?''

"My father told me that there was a time when we were highly regarded, until he angered Mary's father, James. Now she has returned from France, and has continued the slight against our clan. I'll not stand by and let that French king's whore humiliate me.''

"I'm not surprised that you would slander our queen.'' Andrew's words were slurred, and he knew that the pain would soon take him down. ''But even if you spend a lifetime at Court, you'll never be a noble, Logan. You're undeserving of the title.''

Infuriated, Fergus thrust his sword and Andrew managed to duck before coming up behind him. With a viselike grasp on his throat he caught Logan's arm and twisted until the sword dropped to the ground.

"You've broken my arm." Logan's howl of pain had the crowd of onlookers moving closer to form a circle around the two men.

"Do you concede?" Andrew's breathing was labored.

"Aye."

At Logan's whispered words Andrew released him.

The moment he was free Logan turned and butted his head into Andrew's chest, driving him backward. As soon as his opponent was down he leapt on him and began pummeling him about the face until Andrew's eyes were swollen shut.

"An old trick my father taught me," Logan muttered. "I had no intention of conceding, you fool. I simply do whatever it takes to win, even if that means lying, cheating and taking advantage of my enemy's weakness. And your greatest weakness is that honor you wear like a badge.'' His hands closed around Andrew's throat and he began to squeeze. "You've no more strength left to fight me. Now will you taste my vengeance."

Gwenellen, nearly crushed in the arms of Logan's

warrior, was forced to stand by and watch as Andrew slid closer and closer to death. His face was bloodied beyond recognition. His strength throughout this ordeal had been unbelievable, but she could see that his wounds were taking their toll. Though his will remained strong, his body was quickly failing him.

"Oh, Andrew." Her cry seemed to stir him momentarily. "Please, my love. You mustn't die."

The sound of her voice wrapped itself around his heart. What would happen to her if he failed? It was more than he could bear to contemplate.

Calling upon every ounce of strength he possessed, he gripped Logan's hands and managed to pry them loose. With a snarl Logan curled his hand into a fist. Before he could make contact Andrew rolled aside, and heard his opponent's grunt of pain as his fist encountered hard-packed earth instead.

There was a ripple of approval from those around them. Even Logan's warriors seemed to be silently cheering for the man who refused to die.

Andrew staggered to his feet and stumbled backward.

As Logan got up and started toward him, several in the crowd began to murmur aloud.

"That's it, m'laird. Don't let him get too close."

"Stay on ye'r feet, m'laird. Ye mustn't fall now or he'll be on ye like a dog."

"He's a coward, m'laird. Afraid to fight ye with

just his fists. Watch now. A show of strength and he'll run.''

Their words were lost on Andrew. All he could hear was a strange buzzing sound in his head. All he could feel was pain. Still, all his training as a warrior had taught him to focus completely on the enemy.

Fergus Logan came into his line of vision, and he heard the ripple of voices raised in alarm a moment before he saw the glint of a knife in Logan's hand, which he'd retrieved from the grass.

''Too weak to fight me without help, Logan?'' His taunt, spoken between bloody lips, had his opponent lunging.

This time Andrew was ready. He planted his feet, determined to absorb the blow. As Logan swung the knife in an arc, Andrew's hand clamped around his wrist and twisted. The two men fell in a heap and began rolling over and over in the grass.

While the crowd watched and waited in breathless silence, the two men went as still as death. Finally Fergus Logan pushed himself up and took a halting step toward Sabrina, who was still astride her mount.

Her smile was dazzling. ''Go back and fetch him, for you promised me that Andrew Ross would kneel before me this day.''

''Aye. But I…'' His words trailed off.

The villagers gasped as a breeze rippled his tunic, revealing the hilt of his knife protruding from his chest.

He took another step toward Sabrina, then suddenly dropped to his knees before falling prone before her. As he gasped his last breath, blood spilled from the wound and soaked the ground beneath him.

The air rang with the cheers of the villagers as they watched their enemy fall, and the shouts from Logan's warriors as they milled about in search of a leader to tell them what to do.

"Attack, you fools," Sabrina shouted.

"But we have no leader, my lady," a brawny warrior called.

"I will lead you now. These peasants are no match for our strength. We must kill them. All of them." Seeing some of Logan's warriors running toward the shelter of the nearby forest, she cupped her hands to her mouth. "Kill any man, even our own, who attempts to flee."

The warrior holding Gwenellen released her as he struggled to slip his sword from the scabbard. Gwenellen used that moment of distraction to rush to Andrew's side.

Her heart nearly stopped as she cradled the limp, bloodied body in her arms. "Oh, my beloved. Please, Andrew. Speak to me."

Just then there was the sound of thunderous hoofbeats, and an army of Highlanders wearing the Ross plaid appeared over a rise in the meadow. With the sound of bagpipes from the rear of their column, they approached, causing Logan's warriors to turn and flee, with Sabrina in the lead.

A tall, handsome warrior caught the housekeeper in a fierce hug and listened as she relayed to him all that had happened. Then, with his arm firmly around her waist he approached the place where Gwenellen knelt still holding Andrew in her arms.

"My lady, I am Drymen MacLean. My wife has told me of Logan's treachery. I've sent my men in pursuit of his woman and his warriors."

When she didn't respond he knelt beside her. "My lady. Did you hear me?"

She looked up, tears streaming down her cheeks. "Forgive me, sir. I'm most grateful that you're here. But I fear it's too late to save Andrew." Her shoulders shook with uncontrollable sobs. "He is lost to us."

Chapter Twenty

"Here now, my lady." Mistress MacLean caught Gwenellen's slumped shoulders and helped her to her feet, while Drymen lifted the body of his laird in his arms and began the trek to the castle, with the villagers trailing behind.

It was a solemn procession that wound its way across the meadow, through the garden, and into the castle.

Once inside, the housekeeper pointed a finger. "We'll lay the laird out in the great hall."

Before her husband could do as she asked, Gwenellen stopped him with a hand on his sleeve. "Nay. Take him to the library in the old abbey."

"But, my lady…" The housekeeper's protest died when she saw the tears shimmering in Gwenellen's eyes.

When her husband looked to her for direction, she gave a brisk nod of her head. Sucking in a breath she straightened her shoulders. "I'll go ahead with some of the servants and have a fire started. It will take some goading, but I'm sure we can persuade the villagers to put aside their fears long enough to do their duty by the laird."

By the time Drymen and Gwenellen stepped into the room there was a fire burning on the hearth, and the chaise was draped in furs. The warrior gently settled his laird in the nest of fur before taking a step back. "The people will want to pay their respects."

Gwenellen nodded, grateful for this man's quiet strength.

As he took his leave, his wife approached with a basin of water and several linen squares. "I'd like to clean him up, my lady, before the people see him."

"Thank you, Mistress MacLean. I'll do it."

"It won't be an easy thing to see his wounds, my lady."

"Nay. It won't be easy. But what he did was so brave, how can I do less? I need to do this, don't you see?"

"I understand." The housekeeper stood a minute, watching as Gwenellen wrung out a cloth and began to wash the blood. Then with a sigh she turned away and began directing the servants. "I'll need a fresh tunic and plaid for the laird. Ale for the warriors. And a meal laid out in the great hall for the villagers who will no doubt remain through the night."

There was a flurry of footsteps as the servants scattered. And then there was only silence as Gwenellen bent to the gruesome task of cleaning the body of the man she loved.

The man she loved.

Her hands stilled, and she felt a fresh round of tears building.

"Oh, Andrew. I never thought to find love here in this place. I foolishly thought your world a place of hatred and fear. A place of hunger and cold. Of chaos and bloody battles. It is all that, but it's also a place of goodness and great kindness. A place where people work together to overcome whatever obstacles lie in the path of life's journey. A place of laughter and love and such incredible joy." Tears spilled over and trailed down her cheeks. "I would have been content to remain in this place forever, as long as you were here with me. But now…" She covered her face with her hands and began sobbing. "Now I can't bear the thought of being here without you."

"Nor…I…without…you, Imp."

At the raspy, whispered words her tears fell faster. "I thought it a blessing to be able to speak with those who have crossed to that other world. But now I know it to be a curse." Blinded by tears she dipped the cloth in water and began scrubbing viciously at the blood that stained his chest.

"Burns…like…fire…of…hell."

"You see? How can I bear to hear your voice and not be able to hold you? To love you? Oh, Andrew, what am I to do without…?'' She went very still as the meaning of his words dawned on her. ''But it can't hurt you now. You're beyond pain.''

''Someone neglected…to tell the pain.''

''Andrew?'' She studied his eyes, tightly closed. Did the lids flicker? She lay a hand on his chest. Did it give a feeble movement? Or was she imagining it?

She pressed her ear to his lips. There. The smallest hint of a breath. Anxious now, she listened to his chest. Was that a heartbeat? Aye, she was certain of it. Though it was feeble, thready, it was a sign of life.

''Oh, Andrew.'' She threw her arms around him and felt him flinch in pain.

''Help me, Imp.''

''I'll do whatever I can, my love.'' Desperate, she looked around for some guidance. ''Father. Can you summon Mum and Gram?'' Hearing no response she called, ''Morgan Ross. Please wake the holy women who dwell in this place.''

In the silence that followed she whispered, ''I know you're here, for I feel your presence. I know so little about healing. Please show me what to do.''

There was a shimmer of light, and then, as it began to take shape, she recognized Morgan Ross standing beside her.

Her eyes glistened with fresh tears. ''He's alive, my laird. Your son is alive.''

''Aye, lass. I told you he was a warrior.''

"You must show me what to do to help him."

"I've brought the finest healers I know." Light began shimmering all around them, and Gwenellen watched as robed women took up positions around the chaise. Then she spotted her father standing just behind her, peering over her shoulder at the man who lay as still as death on the chaise.

"Father." She gave a sigh of relief. "I knew you'd come."

"How could I not, my daughter? And I've summoned help."

There came a sound as of a great rush of wind, and Nola and Wilona appeared, their jewel-colored gowns billowing about them.

"Oh, Mum. Gram." Gwenellen fell into their arms and embraced them fiercely before turning to the shadowy figures who had gathered around. "I ask your help, for Lord Andrew Ross hovers near death."

"You need not fear death, lass." One of the holy women spoke for the others. "If this man has lived an honorable life, his time in eternity will be a time of great peace."

"You don't understand." Gwenellen chewed on her lip to keep it from trembling. "I don't think I could bear losing him so soon after discovering just how I feel about him."

Her mother placed a hand on her arm. "And just what do you feel about this mortal?"

Gwenellen looked at her mother, then turned to her grandmother. "I love him more than I thought it was possible to love another. I will do whatever it takes to save him."

"Oh, my darling." Wilona drew her granddaughter close and pressed a kiss to her temple. "We'll do what we can. And with so many willing to help, it may be possible to spare the life of this Highlander."

The two women joined hands before turning to Gwenellen. "Since you are the only one who can see and speak with the spirits, it will be up to you to let us know when the circle is complete."

Gwenellen watched as the shimmery figures of the holy women grasped hands, then were joined by Morgan Ross, and finally by Gwenellen's own father, who held his wife's hand in his with all the tenderness of a caress.

Though she couldn't see him, Nola felt the whisper of his touch and arched a brow at her daughter, who smiled and nodded.

"It's Father, Mum. He stands beside you, just as he has since he left our world." Gwenellen stepped between Morgan and her father, and took hold of their hands. "The circle is now complete."

Nola and Wilona began to chant the ancient words. Soon the others joined them, lifting their voices to the heavens as they called for healing.

When at last their voices faded, Andrew opened his eyes. Though he was aware of the presence of others in the room, the only one he could see was the honey-haired beauty who walked slowly toward him and dropped to her knees beside the chaise.

Her voice was little more than an awed whisper. "You're alive."

"So it would seem. Though, for a little while, I was not here. I was in a place of great light and peace. But I heard your voice, Imp, and knew I couldn't find joy in an eternity spent without you." He sat up, and waited for the dizziness to pass. Then he touched a hand to the places where he'd been mortally wounded. There was no pain. There were no marks. And though it made no sense, he knew that what he had experienced was beyond the realm of anything in this world. "Were you harmed, my love?"

My love. The words trickled over her taut nerves like a soothing balm. "A few cuts. I'll have my mother heal them before she takes her leave of your world."

Andrew looked beyond her to the beautiful women who stood side by side, watching and listening in silence. "You are Gwenellen's mother and grandmother?"

"We are." Nola led her mother closer, and the two women smiled at him. "It seems you have captured my daughter's heart."

He got to his feet and caught Gwenellen's hand, marveling at the sudden rush of heat. "I'm not sure who is the captive and who is the conqueror. But this I know. She is the sunshine that brought light to my darkness. She is the joy that has replaced my sorrow and anger.'' He turned to Gwenellen and lifted a hand to her cheek. ''If you could find it in your heart to take pity on me, my love, I would ask a favor.''

Gwenellen's heart was pounding. ''Ask it, my lord. I would grant you any favor within my realm.''

''I have no right to ask you to turn your back on the paradise you have described as your home. But if you leave me, the darkness and despair will return and seem all the worse, now that I've felt your warmth and light. My beloved Imp, I beg you to stay in this place and be my wife.''

Gwenellen brushed aside the mist that sprang to her eyes. There would be no tears on this joyous occasion.

Seeing them he was quick to add, ''I know not what the future will bring. It could be danger, destruction, death. But I give you my word that I'll do all in my power to shield you from the hardships of my world. And though I can't promise you paradise, I can promise you undying love.''

She gave him a dazzling smile. ''It's true that the Mystical Kingdom is a paradise. But without you, my love, it would seem a beautiful, empty prison. As for the future, I'll not worry about what is to come. For now, for the time we have together, I'll be content with the knowledge that I have the love of the finest man I've ever known.''

He gave her a quick, heart-stopping smile. ''You'll stay?''

''How could I leave you, when I've found my heart's delight?''

He drew her close and pressed his mouth to a tangle of hair at her temple. ''We'll send for the village priest, and be wed in the abbey as soon as my warriors return.''

Gwenellen's smile faded. ''I understand your wish to be wed in front of the villagers, for you are laird. But I very much desire to have my sisters and their family, as well as Jeremy and Bessie witness our wedding as well.''

Wilona touched a hand to her granddaughter's shoulder. ''It is possible to do both in the space of but a single heartbeat.''

Gwenellen's eyes widened. ''Of course. What was I thinking? You'll see to it?''

''I will, my darling.''

While Andrew watched in astonishment, the older woman lifted her arms heavenward and began to chant. He and Gwenellen were suddenly floating high above the earth, soaring over forests and mountains, meadows and villages, until they drifted gently to earth.

When he looked around they were standing in a meadow much like the one in his Highlands. Clustered around a tidy cottage were two handsome warriors wearing the distinctive plaid of their Highland clans, and two beautiful women who could only be the sisters Gwenellen had described.

She fell into their arms and embraced them before introducing them to Andrew.

She caught the arm of a beautiful, fiery-haired woman with green eyes and a beguiling smile much like her own. "This is my sister Allegra." She linked her arms through those of a tall warrior and a fair-haired lad. "And her husband Merrick, and son Hamish."

Then she beckoned a raven-haired woman and tall, handsome man to her side. "This is my sister Kylia, and her husband Grant."

While Andrew acknowledged the introductions, Gwenellen was embraced by a hunched old woman, and then by a tiny man in a frock coat and top hat. There was such warmth and affection in her voice as she introduced Bessie and Jeremy.

The old woman seemed pleased to see her young friend, but the little troll appeared crestfallen when he heard that she'd returned home to wed a Highlander. "You mean you're leaving me alone here?" His croaks turned to sad little hiccups. "What shall I do without my best friend? Without your sunny smile to cheer me, and your reckless spells to add adventure to my days?"

Gwenellen knelt down and caught his hands in

hers. "Andrew and I will visit often, Jeremy. I promise."

"You will?" His smile returned. "And we'll ride Moonight and Starlight together?"

"Aye." She glanced at the winged horses grazing nearby, and saw Andrew's astonished look as Jeremy and Hamish climbed on their backs and were lifted above the treetops, where fairies flitted in the tallest branches.

Allegra and Kylia caught their younger sister's hands and began leading her toward a tidy cottage in the distance. When Andrew looked alarmed, they merely smiled.

Merrick dropped an arm around Andrew's shoulders. "Have no fear, for it's some sort of woman ritual."

"Aye." Grant nodded in agreement. "They're determined to hear all about their youngest sister's adventure in your land while they prepare her for her wedding."

"What should I do?"

Nola lay a hand gently on his arm. "You can walk with me and see something of the Mystical Kingdom while you tell me about yourself and your people." Her smile was warm and welcoming. "I yearn to know all about the man who has captured the heart of my wild and reckless youngest daughter."

Epilogue

"This Highlander, Andrew Ross, makes you happy?" Allegra studied her sister's reflection in the looking glass as she finished brushing her hair.

"Happier than I ever dreamed I could feel." Gwenellen sighed as Kylia began to tuck sprigs of wildflowers here and there in her curls.

The two sisters stood back to admire their handiwork.

"Oh, Gwenellen." Allegra brushed a tear from her eye. "You seem so different."

"Aye. All grown up." Kylia linked her fingers with those of her little sister. "Mum told us that you have at last found your gifts."

Gwenellen nodded. "I truly can converse with those who have left this world." Her voice took on a dreamy note. "I often saw and spoke with Father here in the Mystical Kingdom, but I thought it was merely because we were so closely connected. But when I arrived in Andrew's castle, I saw and spoke with his father, as well as all those who had been killed by his enemy. It gave me a great deal of satisfaction to know that I could use my gift for some good, for I was able to carry messages to their loved ones."

Allegra smiled. "And you mastered the art of flying."

"Aye. Not just for myself, but an entire village." Gwenellen laughed. "I wish you could have seen it. It was the most amazing sight."

"And now you're to be wed to your Highlander. Are you certain you can be content to spend a lifetime as Andrew's wife?" Allegra saw how her sister's eyes softened at the mention of his name.

"I want nothing more than that. Of course," Gwenellen added with a smile, "there's always his library, if I should find myself restless for a bit of magic. It's filled with the spirits of holy women and books brimming with spells and chants."

Her two sisters glanced at each other and rolled their eyes.

"Heaven help the people of Andrew's village," Allegra muttered as she linked hands with her sister.

Together the three made their way to the meadow, where the others were waiting.

As they drew near, Andrew drank in the sight of his golden-haired pixie in a gown of gossamer gilt that drifted about her ankles with each step. When at last she stood before him, he had to reach out and touch her, to assure himself that she was real.

The others gathered around, forming a circle, while Wilona stretched out her arms over their bowed heads.

"First you two must speak those things that are in your hearts."

Andrew lifted Gwenellen's hands to his lips. "Before you came into my life, I had grown weary of the lying, the cheating that seemed so much a part of my life. I'd foolishly pledged my heart to a woman who had no regard for anyone except herself. A woman who used me to get to my father, in order to satisfy the evil plot of our enemy. When I discovered the death and destruction of all those I loved, I believed that vengeance was my only choice. Then you came along, my beloved imp, and taught me to smile again. And finally to trust. I love you, Gwenellen, more than life itself. And I pledge to you this day my heart and soul. If called upon, I will lay down my life to keep you safe from harm."

Gwenellen looked down at their joined hands, and then up into his eyes. "Before meeting you I cared only about measuring up to my sisters. I felt like a failure because I'd made so many missteps. I thought, when first we met, that it had all been another terrible misstep. But now I know that there are no mistakes. They are merely lessons to be learned. And I've learned the greatest lesson of all. Love can be found when you least expect it. In the midst of death and destruction, love can begin like a tiny seed on barren soil. A seed that grows until it becomes a beautiful fragrant flower. I love you, Andrew Ross, as I have never loved another. To you I pledge my heart, my soul, my love for all time.''

While the others linked hands, Wilona touched the bowed heads of the couple who stood before her. ''From this moment, you are no longer mortal and witch, but are one, joined in love. The bonds that secure you cannot be broken by time or space. Not even death will separate you, for you are bound for eternity. Go now to dwell in the land of the Highlands. But return often to our Mystical Kingdom, to renew and refresh yourselves.''

There was the rustle of a breeze, and Gwenellen and Andrew were lifted into the air, watching those on the ground receding until they were mere specks in the heather.

As they floated past villages and skimmed over forests and mountains, they were able to see the beauty of the Highlands. The power and majesty of the land left them breathless.

They dropped gently into the library of Ross Abbey, where the entire village had assembled.

Andrew glanced in surprise at Gwenellen. ''How can this be? Haven't we been gone for days?''

She shrugged. ''Days. Hours. Mere minutes. It matters not in the Mystical Kingdom. When we left,

Mistress MacLean had been told to prepare for the wedding of the laird. Look.'' She pointed to the priest, who stood in full vestments before the assembled.

As she and Andrew started up the aisle, she heard the whispers of good wishes from those who had died. Though it brought a quick tear to her eye, it brought a smile as well. And then, as a harp played, she saw the robed women standing in the knave, singing with the voices of angels. A song for her ears alone.

She and Andrew paused before the priest and she felt a misty dampness on her arm. Turning she saw her father standing beside her. When she glanced over at Andrew, she saw his father beside him. The old laird winked, and she couldn't hold back the little laugh that bubbled forth.

Andrew closed a hand over hers. ''You're happy, my love?''

''I am. And you?''

''My heart has never been so light.''

After repeating their vows, they turned to greet those in attendance. While Andrew nodded toward Drymen MacLean and his wife, Gwenellen was smiling at the thousands of souls that had filled every bit of space in the abbey, craning for a look at the woman who could see and speak with them.

She'd thought her gift a foolish one. Now she realized that it was a rare and wonderful gift, and one she would treasure for a lifetime. As she would treasure the love of this noble warrior who had captured her heart.

As they moved among the celebrants, Andrew paused to brush a kiss over her lips. "I can't wait until we're alone later, so that I can offer you a proper welcome home, my love."

Home. Aye, her heart whispered. She smiled at the image of her father and Morgan Ross standing to one side, beaming their approval. The Mystical Kingdom was a haven, a paradise, where she would return often to renew and refresh herself. But this place, this man, and his people, were now truly her home. For now. For all time.

*　*　*　*　*

*If you've enjoyed this thrilling tale,
turn the page for a taste of
some of our upcoming
Harlequin Historical romances....*

Chapter One

Julia, Lady Carrington, paused in the door of Thérèse Blanchot's richly appointed saloon, her legs suddenly shaky. There was no reason to be so appre-
hensive; she had merely to find Lord Thayne and, at
the appropriate time, abduct him.

She glanced around the elegant room, its colours
muted reds and golds. Already the saloon was
crowded with patrons. Both men and women fre-
quented Thérèse's saloon, where the suppers were
superb, the guests carefully chosen and the stakes
high. Admittance was by invitation only. Many of
the women chose to come masked, although Julia
had no trouble recognising the Duchess of Langston
at the EO table—but perhaps that was because she
took no trouble to hide her flaming red hair or dis-
guise her husky laugh. Julia's own hair was a muted
brown and completely unremarkable. Not that she

was likely to be recognised at any rate; since her return to England she rarely graced London society.

She moved into the room and looked more closely around, hoping to spot Thayne. But there was no sign of his tall, broad-shouldered figure. Or of a man with tawny brown hair that glimmered with gold. Thérèse had sent word he would be here tonight. Perhaps he was in one of the private parlours. It would be too awful to contemplate if he was to change his mind. She hadn't come up with an alternative plan and she wasn't quite sure if she could work up the courage to do this again.

Thérèse materialised at her side. "My dear, you have arrived. I was not certain you would come." In her early thirties, she was still a beauty with high cheekbones and violet eyes under a crown of thick black hair.

"Yes." Julia took a deep breath. "Is Lord Thayne here?"

"He is. In the gold saloon. However, he is not in the most jovial of moods." Her brow creased with worry. "My dear, I do not know what you have planned, but he is not a man you can cross. If you only would tell me, I could help."

Julia shook her head. "No. I do not want you implicated in any of it." Thayne's hard gaze sprang to mind. She did not want his wrath to fall on Thérèse.

"That does not matter to me." Thérèse hesitated.

"My dear, I wish I could convince you that it is most unlikely he knows anything about Thomas's death.'

"Perhaps not, but he has Thomas's ring. If anything, I want to at least know how it came to be in his possession." She put a reassuring hand on Thérèse's arm. "I will be careful."

"I only want you to be safe."

"I will be. Eduardo is waiting for me outside so I will be well protected."

"Yes." Thérèse still appeared unconvinced.

"Will you take me to him, then? I wish to play a game with him. Perhaps piquet."

"And what then?"

"I will, I hope, have my ring," Julia said lightly. She had no intention of telling Thérèse that she planned to abduct one of her most wealthy and powerful patrons. "And one more thing—I think it would be best if you would pretend you do not know me."

"If that is what you wish. What should I call you?"

Julia frowned. "Jane, I think."

Thérèse's brow shot up. "Jane? Such an ordinary name."

"I am less likely to forget it." She had thought of taking something closer to her own name, Juliana, for instance, but she feared she would blurt out Julia instead. And certainly she did not want him to connect her with anything related to her real identity.

"Then come with me." Theérèse led her through the saloon.

Several patrons greeted Thérèse as they passed but, to Julia's relief, no one gave her more than a cursory glance as they crossed the rich-hued oriental carpet, winding their way among the baize-covered tables. And then she caught sight of someone she knew all too well, her neighbour, Lord George Kingsley. He was hovering near the EO table. The Even-Odd wheel had just been set into motion as Julia and Thérèse passed by. Preoccupied with the spinning wheel, he did not even glance up. Thank goodness for that. If anyone were likely to recognise her under the mask it would be him. She quickly averted her gaze and prayed she could avoid him.

Thérèse stopped in front of the door of one of the private parlours. She looked over at Julia. "Are you certain this is what you wish, my dear?"

Her knees started to shake. She was about to confront the man who perhaps held the only clue to her husband's murderer.

Nicholas polished off the remainder of his brandy in one smooth move and leaned back in his chair. "Another game?" he asked his companion.

Henry Benton gave the pile of vouchers in front of Nicholas a meaningful stare. "No, thank you. Not if I hope to keep my shirt. Believe I'll try my luck at Faro. Dammit, Thayne, I think your wits only sharpen the more you drink.''

Nicholas laughed, but his laugh was hardly amused. ''Then after another bottle or two I should break the bank.''

Benton frowned. ''Don't know why you're drinking like a fish. You'll have the devil of a head tomorrow. If you don't pass out before then.''

''Which is precisely what I plan to do.'' Perhaps in drunken oblivion he'd be able to get through the rest of this anniversary without the images that had haunted him for the past two years.

Benton rose, the frown still on his face. ''Perhaps you'd do best to continue at home.''

''No,'' Nicholas said curtly.

Benton opened his mouth as if to say more, but merely bowed and walked off.

Nicholas slouched back in his chair and reached for the bottle. His hand stayed when he realised someone had entered the small, dim room. He saw Thérèse and then his gaze flickered to the woman with her.

She was of average height and slender. The low-cut silk gown she wore revealed a glimpse of soft curved breasts. She was masked, not an unusual occurrence among ladies of the *ton* who did not wish to be recognised in such a risqué place. She looked vaguely familiar. He frowned and had a sudden recollection of her watching him last evening. Her still, watchful manner had seemed out of place in one of London's most exclusive and high-stake private hells. The thought had crossed his mind that it must be her first time in such an establishment. Apparently he had been mistaken. She looked quite confident as she followed Thérèse towards his table, her eyes behind the mask fixed on his face.

Thérèse stopped, the young woman a little behind her. She clasped her gloved hands in front of her in a way that suddenly reminded Nicolas of a schoolgirl. Thérèse's expression gave nothing away as she addressed him. "Nicholas, may I present Jane? She wishes to play a game of cards with you."

"Does she? I fear I am not in the mood." He would prefer to polish off his bottle in solitude.

"She assures me she is a very skilled player. And she came here specifically to play with you. Surely you do not wish to disappoint her?"

His eyes flickered over the woman. He could think of no reason why she would wish to challenge him. She met his gaze boldly but her saw her fingers tighten around her reticule. So she was nervous. In spite of his desire to remain detached, he felt the faintest stirring of curiosity. "How skilled is she?" he asked.

Thérèse shrugged and glanced quickly at her companion. "I cannot say."

He looked back at Thérèse. "I don't waste my time on amateurs. Tell her I must decline."

The young woman turned her masked gaze on him. "I can hear and speak, my lord." Her voice held more than a touch of annoyance. "And I am hardly an amateur. I never lose." Her voice was low and well bred.

His eyes narrowed. He wondered what the devil she wanted, but there was nothing he could think of. Her voice was completely unfamiliar. "Don't you? Then sit down," he said curtly.

She took the chair across from him. As she sat, he caught a whiff of soft rose. The scent evoked memories he'd prefer to forget. He should undoubtedly send her away after all.

A servant entered the room and spoke to Thérèse. She turned to Nicholas. "I fear I cannot stay. A small crisis with the supper. But I shall be interested in the outcome. My dear," she said to Jane, "I wish you all luck."

Jane nodded and then looked back at Nicholas. He saw her swallow, although the rest of her demeanour was calm.

"What is your game?" he asked.

"Piquet."

"Very well. What odds?"

She looked straight at him. "Anything you wish, my lord."

"Anything?" he asked, his voice suggestive. He allowed his gaze to rest on her lips and then drift down to where her creamy breasts plunged into her bodice. Despite the amount of drink he'd consumed and his indifference, he felt the faint stir of desire.

Her gaze faltered a little. "Anything."

He smiled coldly. This was a new tack—usually women expressed their interest in a more direct fashion and never by challenging him to a card game. "And if I lose?"

She hesitated and then spoke, her eyes on his face. "Then, my lord, you will give me what I wish."

His loins tightened unexpectedly, the thought of what she might want damnably erotic. His eyes went to her lips, soft and slightly parted, and the idea of crushing them beneath his was becoming more enticing by the moment.

What the devil was wrong with him? Apparently he had not consumed enough drink after all. The last thing he should want was a woman, particularly tonight. Except for an occasional one-night liaison, he'd been nearly celibate for the past two years. On the other hand, perhaps a night in a stranger's arms was exactly what he needed to make it through this anniversary. He leaned back in his chair and regarded her through half-closed eyes. "Fair enough. If I lose then I will be at your mercy. However, I would prefer to call you something besides Jane."

"What is wrong? You do not like Jane?" She sounded affronted.

"No. I'd expected something more exotic from

such a woman of, er…mystery. I don't suppose that is your real name?''

''No, but I shouldn't mind if it were.'' She lifted her chin.

He nearly laughed. ''I suppose your given name is something quite extraordinary that makes you long for a name such as Jane.'' He hadn't expected to feel amused.

''No, it is also quite ordinary.''

''Mary? Elizabeth? Harriet?''

''No. Perhaps we should start the game, my lord.'' Now she sounded cross as if she hadn't much time to dally with him. Certainly her voice held no trace of flirtatiousness. In spite of himself he was beginning to feel rather intrigued.

He picked up the cards. Her gaze was suddenly riveted on his hands. ''I assure you I've no intention of cheating,'' he said. ''And if I did, watching my hands with such concentration would not reveal a thing. But if that worries you, you may deal the cards.''

She looked up and smiled, although her smile appeared forced. ''I am not worried about that at all, my lord. I was merely curious about your ring. It is quite unusual.''

''Yes,'' he said curtly.

''Where did you get it?''

His brow snapped together. ''It was given to me.''

''Indeed. By someone close to you?''

"It is, my dear, none of your concern. I believe you expressed a desire to play a game with me." He pushed the cards towards her.

"Yes." She picked up the cards and he noticed her hand trembled a little. However, her movements as she first shuffled and then dealt the cards were quick and practised.

He made the first move and waited for her countermove. She merely stared at the cards in her hand as if mesmerised. He was beginning to wonder if she was a trifle mad.

"Your play. Although I suggest you do it some time within the next hour. I've no desire to stay here until dawn. Unless you would rather forgo the game and leave now."

Her head jerked up. "Leave?"

"Yes, leave. Together," he added carelessly.

"I..." She caught her lower lip between her teeth.

"Well?" he asked. She still hesitated. What the devil was she playing at? For a woman who wanted to seduce him, she was remarkably reticent. He suspected he was dealing with a complete novice. "Then I will decide. I forfeit the game. Under our terms I am now at your command." He threw down his hand.

She stared at the cards and then looked back up at him. "Oh. Well, yes."

"You seem surprised. Perhaps I misunderstood, but I thought we agreed that if you won I would do what you wish. I assume you had something in mind.''

''Yes.'' She rose, stumbling against the chair a little. ''I would like you to come with me.'' She sounded rather prim.

He stood. ''Would you? Very well, I am at your service, my dear Jane. Although I am curious as to where we are going.''

Her lips parted in a nervous little smile. ''It will be a…a surprise.''

His brow rose. ''Indeed.''

''Yes. So, if you will please come.''

He moved to her side and looked down at her. Her demeanour was hardly that of a seductress—if anything her stiff manner reminded him of a governess. He stepped closer to her.

She nearly jumped away. ''Shall we go, then?''

''Perhaps we should before you change your mind,'' he said drily. ''I must own at this point I am quite curious as to what you want.''

''Oh.'' She hurried from the room as if it was all she could do to keep from running.

He followed her into the passageway and took her arm. Her bones felt delicate under his hand. He pulled her around to face him. ''There's no need for such haste, my dear. Unless you are that eager to have your way with me.''

''No…that is, yes.''

''Are you? Most women who have expressed such

a desire show more, er...enthusiasm for the task.''
He released her arm.

"I fear I haven't much practice," she said crossly.

He folded his arms and leaned against the wall.
"So, why exactly did you decide upon me to im-
prove your skills?"

"I..." She stopped, her eyes fixed on the door of
the parlour next to the one they had just vacated. She
stiffened and then yanked her gaze away. "I would
rather discuss this outside."

He glanced in the direction she had been looking.
Lord George Kingsley and Carleton Wentworth had
stepped out of the room. He looked back at her. "I
see. You wish to converse with me in private. Then
let us depart. I am agog with curiosity."

She threw one last glance at the two men and
dashed across the hallway to the staircase. He caught
up to her just before she started to descend. "There
is no need for such haste. I am yours until dawn."

She gave him a startled look. "Oh. Yes, of
course."

He nearly laughed then. He took her arm again
and started down the stairs. He led her to the small
front parlour where they waited for the footmen to
fetch her cloak. She stood near the door, her posture
stiff as if she were about to flee. He came to stand
in front of her and then lifted her chin with gentle
fingers. "You need a few lessons in the art of se-
duction."

"I…" Her lips parted and even in the lamplight he could see colour suffuse her face. A shaft of desire, hot and fierce, pierced him at his maidenly response. He found himself wanting to push her up against the wall and begin the lesson now. He dropped his hand and backed away. He was beginning to think that she was perhaps a most accomplished seductress after all.

They stepped into the foggy London night, the brisk air cooling his cheeks. It also had the effect of clearing his mind. He glanced down at his companion. She now wore a long, rather unfashionable cloak which hid her figure, but he could see the material was of good quality. What was she exactly? A demi-mondaine? But her speech and carriage were those of a well-bred lady and even in her nervousness she had not slipped into other less refined accents. "Well?" he asked. "Where to?"

"We will go to my carriage," she said firmly.

They walked in silence along the fog-shrouded street. But when they turned the corner of the square on to a dark, nearly deserted side street his hackles rose. Although he heard nothing he had the prickling sensation of being watched.

His companion apparently noted nothing amiss. She halted next to a carriage. "We are here, my lord." Her voice was quite calm. Too calm.

His fingers closed around her arm in a tight grip. "So, what exactly do you want, my dear?"

She stared up at him, the dark and the mask completely hiding her expression. "You."

"I think, then, we had best be certain." He yanked her to him, his mouth crashing down on hers in a merciless kiss. She froze and then began to struggle. He released her abruptly.

She stepped back, stumbling a little. Her hand dipped into her reticule. "Please get in the carriage."

He stared at her, then his eyes dropped to the pistol pointed a few inches away from him. "What the devil?"

"I am abducting you, my lord."

"Are you?" He gave a short, surprised laugh. "Are you that desperate? My dear, after that kiss such measures are hardly necessary. I would be more than happy to oblige you without the use of force." His eyes roved over her figure.

"Get in, please, or I will be forced to shoot you." Her voice was still polite, as if she had just requested he take her in to supper at a ball.

"Can you really use that thing?" he asked carelessly.

"Yes." She motioned with the pistol. "Will you just get in?"

"No please this time?" His mouth quirked. "I will if you kiss me again."

"I did not kiss you the first time!" she snapped. "Get in."

He raised a brow. "I don't think so, my dear."

He made a lunge for the pistol and she jumped back.

He felt a blow to the back of his head, and the next thing he knew he was pitching forward.

Julia stared at the man sprawled at her feet, then looked up to see Eduardo.

Eduardo gave her an apologetic look. "Thought I'd best step in before you decided to shoot the lad. Didn't want a scene. You'd best get the ring. What do you want me to do with him?"

"Put him in the carriage, if you please."

He stared at her for a moment and then nodded. "And then…what?"

"I…I want to take him back to Foxwood. I need to find out where he got the ring."

"Very well."

He glanced over at the coachman who had been watching with a disinterested look. "Come on, lad, we'll put him in the coach for the Countess and bind him up good and tight. A pity, however, he isn't a less robust man."

"Yes, 'tis a shame," Julia said weakly. Her legs were beginning to shake. She watched while they managed to bundle Thayne in the carriage, worried Eduardo might have hit him too hard. But then he groaned and let out a string of curses and she almost wished Eduardo had hit him harder.

She stood by the carriage, her nerves on edge,

praying no one had seen the assault. There was only one other coach on the other side of the street, but it was doubtful the coachman could have noticed anything. When they finished, she finally climbed in the carriage and took the seat opposite him. Guilt assailed her when she saw they had not only bound her prisoner, but had gagged him with his cravat as well. She leaned back against the uncomfortable cushions and closed her eyes. Whatever had she done now? She just prayed they would make it to Foxwood without incident.

Brunton watched the carriage turn a corner. They had been following it since it left the French woman's gaming hell. From all appearances, the carriage was about to leave town. He cursed, causing his horse to startle.

Smithers urged his horse next to Brunton's. "Now what? They're leaving town."

"Yes." Brunton scowled. He'd not figured this into his plans. He'd anticipated either waylaying Thayne in a dark street and nabbing the ring or, if he had to, ambushing him while the Viscount rode his big grey through Hyde Park in the early-morning hours. When Thayne had entered Madame Blanchot's he'd been certain his opportunity was at hand. Until Thayne had left with the masked woman. He'd followed them down the street and around the corner. They had stopped in front of a carriage but, instead of climbing in, had seemed to be arguing. Brunton had been forced to dodge across the street when a large, burly man had suddenly appeared out of nowhere and had stopped to watch the two as well. Brunton hadn't actually seen Thayne enter the carriage, but when it had finally rumbled away Thayne and the woman were gone. The burly man now sat on the box next to the coachman. A glimpse of the masked woman in the window of the carriage confirmed she was inside. And, unless Thayne had vanished into the air, he was in the coach as well.

"Don't think the guv'nor will be pleased if he gets away," Smithers said.

"No." Never idle, Brunton's brain latched on to an alternative plan. A slow smile crossed his face. "But he won't. We'll hold them up."

Smithers grinned, showing several blackened teeth. "Always wanted to be a highwayman."

"Keep your wits about you. If we snuff out Thayne the guv'nor will have our heads."

"Thayne won't argue with this." Smithers patted the pistol at his side. "Dare say he'll be occupied with the wench."

Brunton grinned. "We'll hope she keeps 'im busy enough so he'll not notice us."

Chapter One

April, 1889
Indian Territory

Rafe Hunter lifted his hand to bring his patrol of soldiers to a halt. His roan gelding, Sergeant, shifted impatiently beneath him, anxious to return to Fort Reno and the anticipated bucket of grain in his stall. Rafe panned the rolling plains that stood knee-high in waving grass then glanced toward the tree-lined creek that meandered southeast.

It was hard to imagine that in a little over a week this peaceful countryside would be the site of the nation's first Land Run. He had the unenviable task of guarding the western boundary to the two million acres of free land. It was his responsibility to ensure would-be settlers didn't jump the gun and sneak in to stake their claims prematurely.

In addition, it was his duty to keep a watchful eye

on the Cheyenne-Arapaho reservation near the garrison. The extra obligation of gathering up trespassers demanded long days and stretched his company of soldiers to the limits.

When Rafe glanced over his shoulder, his longtime friend—and second in command—lifted a questioning brow. "A problem, Commander?"

"No, just taking time to appreciate the peaceful moment before all hell breaks loose," Rafe replied.

Micah Whitfield grinned wryly. "By the end of the month, I wonder if any of us will recall what *peaceful* feels like."

Rafe stared past Micah to focus on the five prisoners the patrol had flushed from the nearby creeks. The Sooners—as the army referred to the illegal squatters—had illegally set up camp inside the territory, hoping to claim prime property before thousands of anxious settlers could make the Run. After three weeks of relentless patrolling, Rafe and his company of men had a stockade crammed full of Sooners who refused to follow the rules.

To Rafe Hunter a rule was a rule was a rule. Those who broke the rules paid the consequences.

Rafe's attention shifted southeast when he picked up a familiar scent in the evening breeze. Micah must have recognized the familiar scent, too, for he followed Rafe's searching gaze.

"There's more Sooners hunkering down out there," Micah said quietly.

Rafe scowled. "There's always more Sooners scuttling around out there. You capture five and there's another five waiting to take their place. At the rate we're going, we'll have to build another stockade to house them all."

"If you want to make another sweep of the area to determine who started the campfire I'll go with you," Micah volunteered.

"No, you take the prisoners back to the fort," Rafe requested. "I'll reconnoiter the area alone."

"Easier to find the sneaky culprits that way." Micah nodded agreeably. "This patrol makes too much noise. Might as well sound the bugle to announce our arrival. If you locate another camp tonight we can swarm in to surround the intruders first thing in the morning."

While Micah led the patrol back to the fort, Rafe reined his reluctant mount toward the tree-choked creek. Although he was tired and hungry he was determined to rout out another nest of Sooners. By damned, this unprecedented Land Run was going to be fair for all participants—at least if he had anything to say about it.

Rafe dismounted and left his gelding to graze. Employing the Indian-warfare skills Micah had taught him, Rafe moved silently along the creek, following the faint scent of smoke that had caught his attention earlier. To his surprise he spotted a young boy dressed in homespun clothes. Rafe scanned the shadows, expecting to see a crowd of Sooners migrating toward the small campfire. He frowned curiously, wondering if the boy's family had sent him into the territory alone to illegally stake a claim.

The smell of brewing coffee and a simmering pot of beans made Rafe's stomach growl. He had been on patrol all day, wolfing down trail rations for lunch and wearing calluses on his backside. And here was this scrawny kid, tucked discreetly beneath a copse of trees, preparing a tasty meal and lounging by the fire.

It just hit Rafe all wrong. He wasn't going to wait until daybreak to come swarming down with his army patrol. He was going to arrest this kid and haul him back to the fort tonight. Then he was going to seek out this boy's parents and chastise them for sending a child out into the wilderness alone.

He wondered if the kid's family expected a soldier to show leniency and look the other way. It wouldn't be the first time some scheming adult had tried that tactic. But it wasn't going to work with Rafe.

This kid was not going to spend the night, nestled up to the heat of the small campfire, Rafe decided. He was going to find himself wedged into the stockade with the other prisoners. That should teach the kid a lesson he wouldn't soon forget.

Determined of purpose, Rafe circled around the trees to sneak up on the young boy's blind side.

"You're trespassing, son, and you're under arrest," Rafe growled as he emerged from his hiding place.

The kid shrieked in surprise, bounded to his feet and took off through the trees like a cannonball. There was not the usual moment of paralyzed shock, just immediate flight. In addition, the kid was amazingly agile and swift of foot. He zigzagged around the trees like a gazelle.

Scowling at finding himself in a foot race with a kid half his size, Rafe took off at a dead run. "Halt!" he shouted authoritatively.

The boy didn't break stride—just whizzed through the trees and underbrush and never looked back.

Rafe tackled the kid before he could leap over the narrow creek, scramble up the steep incline and disappear in the thick underbrush. He and the boy landed with a splat, and Rafe hooked his arm around his captive's waist.

To his amazement the worming bundle of energy smacked him in the nose with an elbow, squirmed sideways and arched his back. Rafe found himself on the losing end of a mud-wrestling contest before he could blink. The kid was so slippery that he very nearly slithered away before Rafe could grab him by the scruff of his tattered jacket and yank him off balance.

With an enraged squawk the boy fell facedown in the creek. Rafe bounded to his feet and hoisted the kid upright before he took on too much water and drowned.

To Rafe's amazement the waterlogged kid thrust back his leg—and hit Rafe squarely in the crotch. Rafe's knees buckled beneath him, but he kept a death grip on the squirming kid, determined not to let him escape and have to recapture him again.

"Hold still, damn it!" Rafe growled threateningly then gave the kid a good shaking. "You—"

Rafe's voice dried up when the boy's scruffy cap fell off and dropped into the creek. A waterfall of flaming red hair tumbled to the kid's shoulders. "You're a girl!" Rafe croaked in disbelief.

He was still trying to wrap his mind around *that* startling discovery when the female in question ducked her head and plowed into his midsection, causing the air in his lungs to rush out in a pained whoosh.

All those lectures—delivered by his grandfather and father—about treating a lady with the utmost respect and consideration flew right out of his head when the woman shoved him back into the creek and tried to use him as a doormat to make her escape.

In all his thirty-three years he had never encountered a female quite like this one. And *this* one was no lady, Rafe decided as he made a quick grab for her ankle. This was a scrappy, two-legged wildcat who knew how to fight dirty and didn't mind utilizing every trick in the book to make her getaway.

Scrappy female or not, she was still an illegal Sooner and it was his job to evict her from the territory, even at the risk of personal injury—which he had already suffered at her hands. His groin was still throbbing like a son of a bitch. His ribs were still tender after she had used her head like a battering ram. Plus, the claw marks she had left on his neck, during their most recent struggle for supremacy, were bleeding onto the collar of his mud-soaked shirt.

"Enough!" he roared as he concentrated all his energy on rolling on top of her and pinning her down in the water.

Rafe's conscience tried to deliver a scathing lecture when he straddled her bucking hips, clamped his hand over her face and held her head under water until she stopped resisting. But his noble conscience relented when she practically bit a chunk out of his hand.

Muttering, Rafe shifted the heel of his hand to her forehead and held her underwater until all the fight went out of her. When she sagged beneath him, as if she were about to succumb to drowning, he wondered if this was another of the many dirty tricks in her surprising repertoire. And sure enough, she began to struggle again, lashing out with her arms and fists, trying to do enough physical damage to unseat him.

Only when Rafe was reasonably certain that he had held her underwater so long that her lungs were about to burst did he grab a fistful of her hair and pull her into a sitting position beneath him. She exploded to the surface like a spouting whale, cocked her arm and tried to punch him in the nose.

Rafe hurriedly shifted sideways so the intended blow connected with air. He jerked her up beside him while she raked that mop of red hair from her eyes. While she struggled to get her bearings Rafe fished into the pocket of his soggy jacket for a length of rope to shackle her wrists. Thankfully, he was able to restrain her before she used those deadly claws on him again.

"You are under arrest," he muttered as he grabbed her elbow and frog-marched her ashore. "What's your name, woman?"

She tilted her chin defiantly, clamped her mouth shut and glowered at him as he dragged her alongside him to fetch his horse.

Ten minutes later Rafe scooped up the woman and plunked her atop Sergeant. Keeping a firm grip on her leg, he swung up behind her. With her hands secured in the middle of her back, her elbows out so she couldn't clobber him in the midsection, Rafe wrapped one arm around her waist to ensure she didn't launch herself off the horse during their jaunt to the fort. Given the battle royal he had just encountered with this female he wouldn't put another escape attempt past her.

"Where did you learn to fight like that?" he asked five miles later.

"In places I'm sure *you* have never been, General," she smarted off.

"Obviously not. Where I come from ladies don't brawl. I have already determined—the hard way—that you're no lady. Furthermore, I'm not a general. I'm the commandant at Fort Reno. *Major* Rafe Hunter."

She twisted in the saddle to flash him a smirk. "You're from back East, right? Uppity accent. Imperious demeanor. Wealth and pedigree, no doubt. Don't you have better things to do than sneak around, assaulting defenseless women?"

"Defenseless?" he hooted. "I can think of a dozen adjectives to describe you, but defenseless isn't on the list."

She fell silent as they approached the post, and Rafe made no further attempt to pry information from her. It rankled that she poked fun at the privileged background that he had spent years trying to overcome. He had prided himself in becoming his own man rather than flitting by on the laurels accorded to him by the illustrious Hunter family name. Rafe had worked damn hard to prove himself capable and responsible to assume command of this military fort. But in one fell swoop, and in a few choice words, this sassy hellion implied that his personal accomplishments were the result of his family pulling strings to land him this position.

When Rafe halted at the hitching post in front of

officers' quarters, Micah was leaning negligently against the doorjamb. Micah's astute gaze drifted over the female captive then focused on Rafe's disheveled appearance. The hint of a smile quirked his lips as he pushed away from the door to assist the captive from the horse.

"Met with trouble, did you?" Micah questioned as he set the woman on her feet then clamped an arm around her elbow.

Rafe watched in amazement when the hellcat—who had tried to claw *him* to shreds—turned a radiant smile on *Micah*. "If that question was directed to me, sir, then the answer is yes. I would like to press charges against your commanding officer for molestation and assault."

Rafe nearly choked on his breath when the woman mimicked his eastern accent and projected an air of ladylike dignity. When Micah's befuddled gaze bounced back and forth between Rafe and the woman, he had the impulsive urge to spout his denial of her outrageous accusations.

"Well?" the woman prompted haughtily. "Don't I have the right to protest such ill treatment, just because Rafe Hunter is the *commandant* of this fort?"

ITCHIN' FOR SOME ROLLICKING ROMANCES SET ON THE AMERICAN FRONTIER? THEN TAKE A GANDER AT THESE TANTALIZING TALES FROM HARLEQUIN HISTORICALS

On sale September 2003

WINTER WOMAN by Jenna Kernan
(Colorado, 1835)

After braving the winter alone in the Rockies, a defiant woman is entrusted to the care of a gruff trapper!

THE MATCHMAKER by Lisa Plumley
(Arizona territory, 1882)

Will a confirmed bachelor be bitten by the love bug when he woos a young woman in order to flush out the mysterious Morrow Creek matchmaker?

On sale October 2003

WYOMING WILDCAT by Elizabeth Lane
(Wyoming, 1866)

A blizzard ignites hot-blooded passions between a white medicine woman and an amnesiac man, but an ominous secret looms on the horizon....

THE OTHER GROOM by Lisa Bingham
(Boston and New York, 1870)

When a penniless woman masquerades as the daughter of a powerful marquis, her intended groom risks it all to protect her from harm!

Visit us at www.eHarlequin.com

HARLEQUIN HISTORICALS®

HHWEST27

PICK UP THESE HARLEQUIN HISTORICALS®
AND IMMERSE YOURSELF IN RUGGED
LANDSCAPE AND INTOXICATING ROMANCE
ON THE AMERICAN FRONTIER

On sale November 2003

THE TENDERFOOT BRIDE by Cheryl St.John
(Colorado, 1875)

Expecting a middle-aged widow, a hard-edged
rancher doesn't know what to do when his new cook
is not only young and beautiful, but pregnant!

THE SCOUT by Lynna Banning
(Nebraska and Wyoming, 1860)

On a wagon train headed to Oregon, an independent
spinster becomes smitten with her escort,
a troubled army major.

On sale December 2003

THE SURGEON by Kate Bridges
(Canada, 1889)

When his troop plays a prank on him, a mounted
police surgeon finds himself stuck with an unwanted
mail-order bride. Can she help him find his heart?

OKLAHOMA BRIDE by Carol Finch
(Oklahoma Territory, 1889)

A by-the-book army officer clashes with a beautiful
woman breaking the law he has sworn to uphold!

Visit us at www.eHarlequin.com

HARLEQUIN HISTORICALS®

Your opinion is important to us! Please take a few moments to share your thoughts with us about your experiences with Harlequin and Silhouette books. Your comments will be very useful in ensuring that we deliver books you love to read.
***Please take a few minutes to complete the questionnaire,
then send it to us at the address below.***

Send your completed questionnaires to:
Harlequin/Silhouette Reader Survey, P.O. Box 9046, Buffalo, NY 14269-9046

1. As you may know, there are many different lines under the Harlequin and Silhouette brands. Each of the lines is listed below. Please check the box that most represents your reading habit for each line.

Line	Currently read this line	Do not read this line	Not sure if I read this line
Harlequin American Romance	❑	❑	❑
Harlequin Duets	❑	❑	❑
Harlequin Romance	❑	❑	❑
Harlequin Historicals	❑	❑	❑
Harlequin Superromance	❑	❑	❑
Harlequin Intrigue	❑	❑	❑
Harlequin Presents	❑	❑	❑
Harlequin Temptation	❑	❑	❑
Harlequin Blaze	❑	❑	❑
Silhouette Special Edition	❑	❑	❑
Silhouette Romance	❑	❑	❑
Silhouette Intimate Moments	❑	❑	❑
Silhouette Desire	❑	❑	❑

2. Which of the following best describes why you bought *this book?* One answer only, please.

the picture on the cover	❑	the title	❑
the author	❑	the line is one I read often	❑
part of a miniseries	❑	saw an ad in another book	❑
saw an ad in a magazine/newsletter	❑	a friend told me about it	❑
I borrowed/was given this book	❑	other: _____	❑

3. Where did you buy *this book?* One answer only, please.

at Barnes & Noble	❑	at a grocery store	❑
at Waldenbooks	❑	at a drugstore	❑
at Borders	❑	on eHarlequin.com Web site	❑
at another bookstore	❑	from another Web site	❑
at Wal-Mart	❑	Harlequin/Silhouette Reader	
at Target	❑	Service/through the mail	❑
at Kmart	❑	used books from anywhere	❑
at another department store or mass merchandiser	❑	I borrowed/was given this book	❑

4. On average, how many Harlequin and Silhouette books do you buy at one time?

I buy _____ books at one time ❑
I rarely buy a book ❑

MRQ403HH-1A

5. How many times per month do you shop for any *Harlequin and/or Silhouette* books? One answer only, please.

1 or more times a week	❑	a few times per year	❑
1 to 3 times per month	❑	less often than once a year	❑
1 to 2 times every 3 months	❑	never	❑

6. When you think of your ideal heroine, which *one* statement describes her the best? One answer only, please.

She's a woman who is strong-willed	❑	She's a desirable woman	❑
She's a woman who is needed by others	❑	She's a powerful woman	❑
She's a woman who is taken care of	❑	She's a passionate woman	❑
She's an adventurous woman		She's a sensitive woman	❑

7. The following statements describe types or genres of books that you may be interested in reading. Pick *up to 2 types* of books that you are most interested in.

I like to read about truly romantic relationships	❑
I like to read stories that are sexy romances	❑
I like to read romantic comedies	❑
I like to read a romantic mystery/suspense	❑
I like to read about romantic adventures	❑
I like to read romance stories that involve family	❑
I like to read about a romance in times or places that I have never seen	❑
Other: _____	❑

The following questions help us to group your answers with those readers who are similar to you. Your answers will remain confidential.

8. Please record your year of birth below.

19 _____

9. What is your marital status?

single ❑   married ❑   common-law ❑   widowed ❑
divorced/separated ❑

10. Do you have children 18 years of age or younger currently living at home?

yes ❑   no ❑

11. Which of the following best describes your employment status?

employed full-time or part-time ❑   homemaker ❑   student ❑
retired ❑   unemployed ❑

12. Do you have access to the Internet from either home or work?

yes ❑   no ❑

13. Have you ever visited eHarlequin.com?

yes ❑   no ❑

14. What state do you live in?

_____

15. Are you a member of Harlequin/Silhouette Reader Service?

yes ❑   Account # _____   no ❑   MRQ403HH-1B

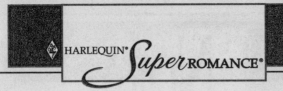
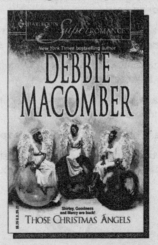

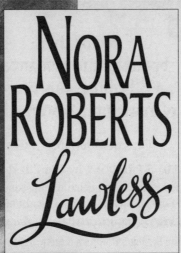

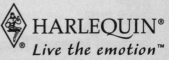

Savor the
breathtaking romances
and thrilling adventures
of Harlequin Historicals®

On sale November 2003

MY LADY'S PRISONER by Ann Elizabeth Cree

To uncover the truth behind her husband's death,
a daring noblewoman kidnaps a handsome viscount!

THE VIRTUOUS KNIGHT by Margo Maguire

While fleeing a nunnery, a feisty noblewoman
becomes embroiled with a handsome knight in a
wild, romantic chase to protect an ancient relic!

On sale December 2003

THE IMPOSTOR'S KISS by Tanya Anne Crosby

On a quest to discover his past, a prince masquerades
as his twin brother and finds the life and the love
he'd always dreamed of....

THE EARL'S PRIZE by Nicola Cornick

An impoverished woman believes an earl is
an unredeemable rake—but when she wins
the lottery will she become the rake's prize?

Visit us at www.eHarlequin.com

HARLEQUIN HISTORICALS®

HHMED33